LEARNING
SUPPORT
SERVICES

Please return
on or before
the last date
stamped below

City College
NORWICH

_ 8 APR 2008

D0488373

The School of Whoredom

Pietro Aretino

Translated by Rosa Maria Falvo,
Alessandro Gallenzi and Rebecca Skipwith

ET REMOTISSIMA PROPE

100 PAGES

100 PAGES
Published by Hesperus Press Limited
4 Rickett Street, London sw6 1ru
www.hesperuspress.com

This translation first published by Hesperus Press Limited, 2003

Introduction and English language translation © Rosa Maria Falvo, 2003
Foreword © Paul Bailey, 2003

Designed and typeset by Fraser Muggeridge
Printed in the United Arab Emirates by Oriental Press

isbn: 1-84391-036-5

CONTENTS

You are about to read a conversation between a mother and her doting daughter that is like no other in literature. It was written in or about 1535, and is in effect a lampoon. The high-minded Platonist dialogue was then in fashion, and Aretino mocks its ideas of self-improvement and exemplary virtue for what he believes they are worth. Perhaps a health warning of sorts is necessary, for if Pietro Aretino has an equivalent in English, it is John Wilmot, Earl of Rochester, the satirical thorn in the flesh of Charles II and his debauched Court, who used words like 'fuck', 'cunt' and 'prick' with wit, inventiveness and an appropriate vigour. Aretino does the same in Italian. Satire is as nothing if it lacks a moral purpose, and that of both Rochester and Aretino is plain to see for those who have the open-mindedness to look.

Nanna, the mother in this constantly surprising dialogue, knows the ways of the world and the tricks of the trade. She is an expert in what Shakespeare has Hamlet call 'country matters'. She wants the best, as all good parents do, for her beloved Pippa. Nanna has a lifetime's experience of men and their curious sexual demands to pass on to the girl who is anxious to lose, and retain, her virginity, and start to earn a living. Pippa must realise that whoredom is an art as well as a craft, and its skills have to be mastered. The lastingly successful whore is required to be a consummate actress, playing the intricate game of love with cunning and panache. It is all a question of working 'miracles', and Nanna has plenty of them at her command. Without 'miracles', a whore's career ends with the fading of beauty and the anticipated ravages of time.

The School of Whoredom is not merely a catalogue of positions – though there are enough of those to intrigue the ever-attentive Pippa and startle the innocent reader. No, its power lies in Aretino's gifts as a storyteller. He is a master of the telling anecdote, the one that reveals as much about the anecdotist as the person whose comic misfortunes she is recounting. There is a wonderfully complicated story at the heart of this book, involving a mean and violent client, a painter named Andrea, who paints a gash on Nanna's face, a friend called Mercurio who administers lint to the fake wound and bandages it, and a charlatan from Naples who – miraculously, of course – removes it for a large sum of money extorted from the guilty abuser, who is now the subject of contemptuous gossip. Nanna, whose days as a courtesan had seemed numbered, can entertain again, once her features are restored to their original, attractive state. Pippa listens, enraptured, to her mother's account of how this wiliest of wily tricks was performed, making each of the tricksters richer with its satisfactory outcome. 'You were a valiant man, Mummy, to perform a feat like that,' she gushes, and Nanna responds, 'We're not at the Alleluia yet', meaning that she has even greater triumphs to relate.

'Whoredom has such a genius for invention,' Nanna reflects, after her daughter wonders why she doesn't run a school to teach people what she has learned. 'I love watching you talk,' Pippa says later, and the reader is left to imagine the gestures Nanna is employing when she remembers the habits and needs of her customers. In a key sequence, the ageing whore explains the necessity of making certain, romantically inclined men jealous. One ruse is accidentally to misplace a forged letter from another ardent suitor so that it just happens to find itself in the hands of the man whose feelings she wishes to inflame. There are dangers and pitfalls to negotiate, because a jealous lover can turn nasty to the point of murder. Nanna is a negotiator par excellence. She remembers the exact wording of the letter that created a very profitable fit of jealousy, and Pippa is impressed once more.

'You could say that a courtesan whose heart pounds for anything other than her purse is like a greedy, drunken tavern-keeper, who, instead of denying himself, eats and drinks what he should be selling,' Nanna counsels, and Pippa, heeding her advice, exclaims: 'You really, really do know everything.' Yet the delightful conceit inherent in Aretino's dialogue is that Nanna, for all her vast experience, is cognisant of the fact that each new day brings with it fresh knowledge to assimilate. A whore cannot rest on her laurels. Life is a matter of chance, and a brothel is a place where certain chances have to be taken and opportunities seized. Nanna may boast, and do so with justification, but there is an element of modesty in her complex nature, which she hopes Pippa will appreciate.

The School of Whoredom is a work of serious comedy. Its author befriended one pope, and risked assassination from another before he reached the age of thirty-five. He was in the business of scurrilous exposure, with hypocrisy in all its manifestations as his principal target. Yet his is not the tarnished soul of the tabloid hack, forever rummaging for information concerning the follies, mostly sexual, of the famous. He is a genuine moralist, in the widest sense, who can detect qualities in an old whore that her lustful clients are blinded to. He sounds the human note, and it is worth listening to. He is known – along with Boccaccio (the name means, literally, 'foul' or 'dirty mouth'), Chaucer, and my revered Rochester – as a celebrator of an aspect of existence that is either ignored or condemned, and will continue to be so for as long as civilisation lasts.

That human note sounds memorably and movingly at the close of *The School of Whoredom*, with Nanna and Pippa taking a well-earned nap. On awakening, the women refresh themselves and resume their conversation. The excited Pippa has had a 'lovely dream around daybreak' and Nanna must wait to warn her of the 'betrayals that come from men's love'. A human note, and a tender one too, for even whores, Aretino hints, can be betrayed.

– Paul Bailey, 2003

INTRODUCTION

While Aretino's two works *Ragionamento* [*Conversation*] and *Dialogo* [*Dialogue*] became known in modern times as *Sei Giornate* [*Six Days*] (in the 1969 Laterza edition by Giovanni Aquilecchia), they are distinctly independent works, quite separate in the way they address two different phases and approaches of the writer's cultural development. *Dialogue* was first published in Venice in 1536 and Aretino claims to have written each of its three days in a day.

In *Conversation*, which preceded the *Dialogue*, the conditions symbolising womanhood – nun, wife, whore – are illustrated through Nanna's personal account of her experiences, and each forms a segment of a tumultuous and sentimental biography. Through her voice and train of thought, Aretino provides a sense of the richness and complexity of contemporary society together with a series of references to the uncertainty of the future, and there is no doubt that the events, places, people and social environs described by Nanna were also those of Aretino himself while he was living in Rome during the Medici papacy. Thus the biography of the courtesan can be seen as coinciding with the personal memoirs of the writer.

Dialogue is a fast-track encyclopaedia of sexual material that refers in principal terms to prostitution: the techniques and perils of the profession, and the pimping and opportunism that surround and support it. Nevertheless we can also appreciate, even without further background, that it is a social and political thesis on two worlds, Roman and Venetian, set in a time of great human, geographic and economic upheaval.

The first day of the *Dialogue* – which here forms *The School of Whoredom* – can be seen as a self-contained unit, following its own logic, but it also begins a conversational journey which eventually leads us to a global definition of its themes and a complete description of the world of prostitution and the various characters who populate it. *Dialogue* as a whole provides us with a treatise on human behaviour, and the author's intention is indicated from the outset in each of its titles: 'Day One: Nanna teaches'; 'Day Two: Nanna recounts'; 'Day Three: Wet Nurse explains'. The reader's attention has shifted from the biographical accounts of the protagonist in *Conversation* to a didactic account of the tricks of the trade, the doctrines, and the entire 'school of whoredom' on the first day of the *Dialogue*. Aretino presents a dazzling show of his technical expertise, and while *Conversation* has a genuinely Roman soul, the *Dialogue*, despite its being set in Renaissance Rome on a summer's afternoon, has a Venetian one – it was written during his long and happy exile to the 'Virgin City', about which he sang endless praises from his privileged residence on the Grand Canal. Together they represent the personal metamorphosis of the author.

Despite the bawdy content of the *Dialogue*, it is Aretino's style, rather than his subject matter, that affords his most controversial effects. Through jest and in earnest he stuns the reader – one is tempted to say 'audience' since his power as a dramatist is no less in evidence than his dexterity as a prose writer – by evoking the vulnerability and dignity of the human condition with the skill of a painter; and he is indeed 'such a painter with words'. Aretino's competence as a writer was recognised outside Italy, and he was a noted intellectual on the socio-political stage of his time, earning, in the space of a few years, a fortune and the prestige of exceptional appointments and the support of important patrons. Yet all this, as he was most bitterly aware, was relatively undervalued when it came to establishing a career of any stable significance, despite the excellence of his craft. His subject matter, the precision of his pen and the incisiveness of his social analysis – hallmarks of a true satirist of any era – kept him at a safe distance from public acceptance and therefore historical commentary. He was, as Aquilecchia coined him, one of the 'new men' who entered the Italian literary scene with the advent of the Bembian reform (so named for Pietro Bembo, 1470–1547), which exercised a tremendous classicising influence in the first half of the sixteenth century, establishing Boccaccio's writings as the model for prose and beginning the Petrarchan movement. Aretino was predisposed, given the favourable social conditions, to anticonformist attitudes.

His iconoclastic social satire is presented with even more vigour in some of his other writings, particularly his letters, where the variety of his lexicon is remarkable. His work in general represents a reaction to the new linguistic-literary elitism of the period and his popular vulgarisms attest to the honesty and precision with which he evoked the very animal truths of which we are all aware. In *The School of Whoredom*, and the *Dialogue* as a whole, set against the contextual backdrop of 'civilised' Renaissance man, Aretino dares to confront our secret understanding of what is all too close to home and better packed comfortably away in the cupboard of social taboos. The reader is privy not only to a private conversation between mother and daughter, but also to a host of personal interpretations that can only come from the most intimate of experiences. The shock factor is a tribute to the power and poignancy of his words – we feel almost as if we were reading a private diary – while he angles the full thrust of his creativity in striking out at the powerful.

In *The School of Whoredom*, Aretino endows his characters with sheer theatricality. Nanna is not only an irresistibly entertaining narrator – she is able to articulate her skills as a shrewd dialectician, dissecting her subject with penetrating logic and listing ever subtler schemes for achieving success. She identifies herself as a veritable 'well' of information, keen to relate what her eyes and ears have witnessed since her days in the monastery, and if prostitution itself offers no guarantees in life, all the social etiquette will nonetheless be of some value to Pippa; hence, the sharp attention to language, clothes, appearances, behaviour, power games, social positioning and other details. While Nanna's speeches are without scruples, perhaps testament to her avarice and the fear of ageing, Aretino is careful to contrast this with Pippa's girlish eagerness, and though the latter is forced to live in times more hostile for whores, she has the advantage of her mother's careful preparation and precious guidance, and so can reasonably hope to make a go of this profession.

Through Nanna, Aretino launches a scathing attack on contemporary scholarship and social pretension, warning Pippa of the arrogance of feigned social graces and favouring simplicity, reiterating the premise that: 'Flattery and deceit are the darlings of great men'. In his anecdotal characters we find the clergyman who often and willingly betrays his mission, the rich who frequently elude the ideals they proclaim, and the rest of society – of which the courtesan is undoubtedly at the lower end, the wicked example par excellence – among whom misery and envy are the chief causes of every type of imbroglio, infidelity and compromise, including prostitution. Everything that would normally hide behind innuendo is made explicit; his writing seems to flow as spontaneously as Nanna's storytelling and backtracking, asserting an absolute lack of interest in any form of linguistic indoctrination. He has a preference for other, more concrete values, which, in Nanna's case, means cold, hard cash.

Aretino's style positively revels in a series of reiterations and crescendos, showing a marked tendency to generalise and classify, and an unquenchable taste for playful, blasphemous and provocative listings. Bursting with sexual metaphors, deformed Latinisms, and Hispanic borrowings, his language includes malicious citations of Dante, Petrarch, Boccaccio and Pulci. Always with parodic intent, he hoards proverbs, colloquialisms, compound nouns and Wellerisms. One can imagine the writer brandishing his pen, as he waxes lyrical through the voice of Nanna, a character who seems both to live and to talk. Indeed, it's the illiterate Pippa who shares and expresses the reader's enjoyment. His descriptions are indeed a visual as well as a philological feast, a banquet to which we are invited, on the proviso that we throw caution to the wind and share in his spirited disdain for convention, just like Nanna's 'old codgers' who are 'the enemies of formality'. Sometimes crude and violent, sometimes allusive, and often lovably confidential, Aretino's writing seems in constant pursuit of caricatured and twisted, even surreal effects. He loves personification and hyperbole, and cultivates alliterations, playing a clever game of juxtaposition on many levels, and demonstrating a hearty appetite for detail in the many vignettes that make up Nanna's lecture.

Perhaps the most distinctive feature of his language is its proliferation of metaphors, especially with erotic terminology; and his comic genius for differentiating the seemingly countless ways of terming male and female genitalia alone saves him from appearing repetitive. Aretino is a master of metaphor, and each one grows from the one before in a virtually endless procession; like a cancan sequence, the images dance uninterruptedly out onto the stage of Nanna's, Pippa's and our imaginations. Aretino is, of course, perfectly aware of his own gifts, making a point of using Pippa as a mouthpiece for their appreciation: 'I wouldn't mind if you kept on for a whole year.'

While the seasoned and masterful ruses employed by Nanna are a far cry from the 'sexy shop' of today's Italy, there is no doubt that this ageless practice was as much about careful marketing, satisfying clients and cutting one's losses then as it is now; Pippa must avoid returning home at the end of the day with 'a full belly and an empty purse'. For a prostitute, sex is always mediated by the requirements of the 'trade', subject to the ruthless laws of survival, and thus almost entirely freed from the mythologies of love and sentimentalism. But there is a difference between the type of whore Nanna wants her daughter to become and the ordinary 'poor wretches' out there, and her long speech on the perils of simply 'planting [oneself] outstretched on the bed' shows her compassion for the misfortunes of those who must pay, inevitably, with their bodies. Here Aretino introduces a moment of reflection, a shadow side, emotive rather than stylistic, bestowing the work and the discourse with an unexpected weightiness and a very real depiction of the pathos of prostitution.

– *Rosa Maria Falvo, 2003*

Note on the Text:

The current text comprises the first 'day' of Aretino's *Dialogue;* it is based on Pietro Aretino: *Ragionamento – Dialogo*, BUR Rizzoli, Milan (1998).

The School of Whoredom

NANNA: What's this fury, this temper, this fever, this frenzy, this anxiety, this badgering and this tantrum of yours all about, you little nuisance?

PIPPA: I'm cross because you won't let me be a courtesan as my godmother, Lady Antonia, advised you.

NANNA: You can't have lunch at nine o'clock, you know.

PIPPA: You're a wicked stepmother, sniff, sniff…

NANNA: Whimper away, my little one.

PIPPA: I certainly will.

NANNA: Forget your pride – forget it, I say, because if you don't mend your ways, Pippa, if you don't mend them, then you won't have anything to cover your arse, because nowadays there are so many whores out there that those who don't work miracles for a living won't make ends meet; and it's not enough to be good-looking, to have pretty eyes and blonde braids; only art or luck will give you the edge, the rest is a waste of time.

PIPPA: If you say so.

NANNA: That's how it is, Pippa, but if you follow my good advice, and if you open up your ears to what my experience can teach you, then lucky, lucky you…

PIPPA: Hurry up and make me a lady, then, I'm all ears.

NANNA: Provided you listen to me and stop fooling around with your head full of nonsense as usual, while I tell you what's good for you, then I swear to God on these Our Fathers I mumble all day long that in a fortnight at the most you'll be on the market.

PIPPA: God willing, Mother.

NANNA: You have to be willing, too.

PIPPA: I am, dear Mummy, precious Mummy.

NANNA: If you are, then I am; and you know, my dear, I'm absolutely certain you'll become greater than any pope's favourite; I see you ascending to heaven – so mind what I say.

PIPPA: I'm listening.

NANNA: Pippa, though I make people believe you are sixteen, you're twenty clear and plain; you were born just after the end of Leo's conclave, and when all Rome was shouting 'Balls, balls!' I was screaming 'Oh God, oh God!' And it was just as the arms of the Medici were being hung on the door of St Peter's that I had you.[1]

PIPPA: Then don't keep me here cooling my heels – my cousin Sandra says they use eleven- and twelve-year-olds all over the world, and that anything else is pretty worthless.

NANNA: I can't deny it, but then you don't even look fourteen. But let's get back to the point: you'll have to listen without daydreaming – imagine that I'm the master and you're a schoolboy learning to read, or if you prefer that I'm a preacher and you're a Christian; if you see yourself more as a schoolboy, then listen to me like he does when he's afraid of getting a thrashing; if you see yourself as the Christian, pay heed the way he does to a sermon for fear of going to hell.

PIPPA: I will.

NANNA: My dear, people who squander money, reputation, in fact their very lives, running after whores, are always moaning about the empty-headedness of one or another of them, as if the whore's stupidity was the thing that's ruining them; and they despise and threaten them, not realising that the fluff they have in their heads is the punter's good fortune. So I've decided that you'll know better: you'll make the poor fellows feel first hand that they'd be in deep trouble if the whores they came across weren't mere thieves, traitors, rogues, fools, dunces, slatterns, scoundrels, wastrels, drunkards, smutty, ignorant, loutish, and the very devil, and worse.

PIPPA: Meaning?…

NANNA: Meaning… that whores don't have as much wit as they have malice, and, when they've put up with it for six, seven or ten years, people eventually wise up because of the treacheries and betrayals they've been subjected to day and night, and send them off to the pillory. And they'd take more pleasure in seeing those whores ruined than they'd take displeasure in watching themselves being cheated. And if some whores are starving, while they carry leprosy, cancer and the French disease[2] at their own expense, it's because they've never spent a single sensible hour.

PIPPA: Now I'm beginning to understand.

NANNA: Listen carefully and fix my sermons and my gospels in your head – they'll make everything clear to you in two words: if a doctor, a philosopher, a merchant, a soldier, a monk, a priest, a hermit, a gentleman, a monsignor or a King Solomon is made to look a fool by the most hare-brained of whores, how do you think a courtesan with an ounce of common sense would deal with those simpletons?

PIPPA: They'd give them a good going over.

NANNA: So, you see, becoming a whore is no career for fools, well I know it, and I won't be hurried in your case; it calls for more than lifting your skirts and saying 'Come – I'm coming', if you don't want to close up shop the day it opens. Anyway, coming to the point, you'll find that, as word goes round that you're on the market, many will want to be first served; and I'll be like a confessor reconciling the rabble, with an earful of 'psst psst' from messengers sent by one man or another, and you'll always be booked by at least a dozen – we'd need there to be more days in the week than there are in a month. But I'll be careful, and I'll reply to such and such a master's servant: 'Yes, it's true that my Pippa let herself be caught once – God knows how (old gossip, bloody gossip, it'll be paid for!) – but my little daughter is purer than a dove and not to blame. Upon my word, she only gave in once, and I won't give her over to any commoner. But Your Lordship has charmed me so much that I can't really say no, so she'll come shortly after the Hail Mary.' And as the envoy gets ready to trot off with the answer, you cut across the house, and pretending your hair has come undone, let it fall onto your shoulders and enter the room, lifting your face just so the fellow can get a glimpse of it.

PIPPA: Why should I do that?

NANNA: Because all servants are frauds and cheats to their masters, and as soon as this one gets home to his master, panting and breathless, to win his graces he'll say: 'Master, I was so clever that I managed to see the girl – she has braids like threads of gold, two eyes that would put a falcon to shame; another thing: I mentioned your name on purpose to watch her reaction – well, she seemed about to burn with a sigh.'

PIPPA: What good will lies like that do me?

NANNA: They'll put you in good favour with your suitor, making every hour he waits for you feel like a thousand years. And how many dupes do you think there are who fall in love from hearing the praises of chambermaids for their mistresses, and whose mouths water while these liars and hoaxers praise them to the skies?

PIPPA: Are chambermaids from the same mould as servants?

NANNA: Even worse. So then you go to the house of this same gentleman, and I come with you. As soon as you get there, he'll come to meet you either at the top of the stairs or maybe even as far as the entrance; compose yourself (as you may have got a bit ruffled on the way), tidy yourself up and sneak a little look at his companions who will, quite reasonably, keep fairly close. Stare humbly into his eyes, and, giving him a scented curtsy, unfurl a greeting the way brides and women in childbed do – according to Perugina – when the husband's relatives or friends touch their hand.

PIPPA: It might make me blush.

NANNA: Which would make me very happy, since the rouge that modesty puts on young girls' cheeks satisfies any soul.

PIPPA: All right then.

NANNA: When the formalities are over, the man you'll be sleeping with will first of all make you sit beside him, and, as he takes your hand, he'll flatter me – I'll be keeping my eyes firmly fixed on you, pretending to be amazed by your beauty, so as to direct the gaze of the guests onto your face. So he'll start to say: 'Madam, your mother has good reason to adore you, since others produce females, and she angels,' and if it so happens that while saying something like that he bends down to kiss your eye or forehead, turn to him sweetly and let out a little sigh that he can barely hear. And if possible make your cheeks go pink at the same time, the way I told you – he'll fall for you at once.

PIPPA: Really?

NANNA: Certainly.

PIPPA: Why?

NANNA: Because sighing and blushing together are a sign of love – they betray the first stirrings of passion; and since everybody else keeps quiet and reserved, the man who's going to enjoy you that night will begin to think you are madly in love with him, believing it all the more as you pursue him with your glances. And as he's talking to you, he'll draw you gradually into a corner, and with the sweetest and most subtle words he can manage, he'll start to chat you up. Here you must answer on cue, and with a soft voice try to say a word or two that don't smack of the brothel. Meanwhile the rest of the group, who've been lingering around me, will approach you like snakes slithering through the grass, saying one thing or another, laughing and teasing. You must keep your head, and whether you're silent or talking, make sure that both speech and silence look pretty on you. And while addressing one or another, glance at them without lewdness, the way observant nuns look at monks. And only the lover who's providing your dinner and lodging should be fed on tempting glances and alluring words. When you want to laugh, don't raise your voice, gaping like a whore and letting them see what's in your mouth, but laugh in such a way that no part of your face looks less lovely; in fact enhance your beauty by smiling and beaming, and sooner let a tooth fall out of your mouth than a dirty word. Don't swear by God or the saints, constantly saying: 'It's not true'. And don't get angry at the remarks of people who enjoy teasing girls like you – pleasant manners and a ladylike appearance are better clothing than velvet for a girl who is constantly at parties. And when you're called to supper, though you should always be the first to wash your hands and make your way to the table, let them call you more than once, because one is exalted by one's humility.

PIPPA: I'll do that.

NANNA: And when the salad arrives, don't rush at it like a cow at hay, but take teeny-weeny mouthfuls, and put them in your mouth without greasing so much as a finger – and don't lower your head, gobbling up the food straight off your plate, as I have seen some oafs do. Keep majestically erect, extending your hand graciously, and when you ask for a drink, do it with a nod of your head. If the decanters are on the table, help yourself and don't fill the glass to the brim – slightly over halfway will do. Bring it gracefully to your lips, and never drink it all.

PIPPA: And what if I'm very thirsty?

NANNA: Even so, only drink a little bit so you don't get a name for being a glutton and a drunkard. Don't eat with your mouth open, chomping annoyingly and messily, but in such a way that you hardly seem to be eating. And while you're having dinner, talk as little as you can, and if others don't question you, make sure the chatter doesn't come from you. If someone at your table offers you the wing or breast of a capon or partridge, accept it graciously, glancing all the same at your lover with a gesture that begs his permission without asking it; and when you've finished eating, don't belch, for the love of God!

PIPPA: What would happen if one escaped me?

NANNA: My God! You'd fall headfirst into the gutter – you'd be finished.

PIPPA: And if I do exactly as you say, and more, what will happen then?

NANNA: You will be renowned as the most talented and gracious courtesan alive, and when people talk about other girls, everyone will say: 'Shut up! The very shadow of Lady Pippa's old shoes is worth more than such-and-such a girl all dolled up'; and those who know you will be your slaves and will go about preaching your virtues, so that you'll be more sought-after than people who behave like rogues and rascals are shunned. And just think how delighted I'll be.

PIPPA: What should I do once we've finished eating?

NANNA: Amuse yourself for a while with the man sat next to you; never leave your lover's side, and when bedtime comes around, let me go back home. Then, having reverently said 'Goodnight, Your Lordships', take more care than with fire not to be seen or heard peeing or easing your bowels, or even carrying a handkerchief to wipe yourself with, because things like that are enough to make a chicken retch – and they peck at all sorts of shit. Having secured yourself in the bedroom, look around to see if there is a piece of linen or a cap that you like, and, without asking, start praising the linen and the caps.

PIPPA: What for?

NANNA: So that the dog, scenting the bitch, will offer you either one or the other.

PIPPA: And if he offers me them?

NANNA: Slip him a kiss with the tip of your tongue, and accept.

PIPPA: I'll do that.

NANNA: Then while he gets straight into bed, you begin undressing very slowly and murmur a few words to yourself adding in some little sighs, so that when you slip in next to him, he'll have to ask: 'My love, why are you sighing?' Then let out another heartfelt sigh and say: 'Your Lordship has charmed me', hugging him tightly as you say it. Kiss him again and again, then make the sign of the cross, pretending you forgot to do it before getting in. And if you don't want to say your prayers or anything, move your lips a little so you appear well mannered in everything you do. Meanwhile the scoundrel, who's been waiting for you in bed the same way someone with a beastly hunger sits at the table before the bread or wine have been brought out, will begin fondling your tits, shoving his entire face in as if to drink from them, and then he'll slide his hands down your body, little by little, to reach your little cunt. After a few little pats, he'll start feeling your thighs, and since your buttocks act like a magnet, they'll soon draw his hand, I can tell you. After playing with them for a bit, he'll wedge his knee between your legs and try to turn you over (not daring to ask for it like that the first time), but you go rigid. Even if he starts whining like a spoilt child, don't turn over.

PIPPA: And what if he forces me?

NANNA: No one gets forced, silly girl.

PIPPA: And why should I make him do it in front rather than behind?

NANNA: Simpleton, you talk just like the fool you are; tell me: what's worth more, a julio or a ducat?

PIPPA: I get you: silver is worth less than gold.

NANNA: That's it. Now I'm thinking of a good trick…

PIPPA: Teach it to me.

NANNA: …a good one, a very good one.

PIPPA: Oh please, Mummy.

NANNA: If he keeps wedging his knee between your thighs, trying to have you his way, feel around to see if he has a bracelet on his arm or rings on his fingers; and while the blowfly is flitting around you, tempted by the smell of the roast, see if he'll let you take them off. If he does, then let him do it, and once you've taken all his jewels, you'll swindle him all right. If he won't let you, say openly: 'So Your Lordship goes in for that nasty stuff?', then he'll take you the right way. And when he climbs onto you, my dear, get down to it. Do it, Pippa, because the caresses that make these jousters come quickly are their downfall, and if you give them the right way, they'll die of pleasure. A whore who can do it well is like a merchant who sells his wares for a high price: the flattery, the games and the titillations of a cunning whore are best compared to a haberdashery shop.

PIPPA: What a comparison!

NANNA: Imagine a shopkeeper who has laces, looking glasses, gloves, diadems, ribbons, thimbles, pins, needles, girdles, bonnets, trimmings, soap, scented oil, Cyprus powder, wigs and a hundred thousand other things. So, in her shop, a whore has sweet talk, smiles, kisses, glances – but this is nothing: in her hands and in her pussy she has rubies, pearls, diamonds, emeralds and the very melody of the world.

PIPPA: How's that?

NANNA: How? There isn't a single man who doesn't touch heaven when the woman he's making love to, while slipping in a tongue-kiss, grabs his thingy, squeezing it two or three times, making it stand erect, and stiff as it is, gives it a little shake, making his mouth water. Then, just a few moments later, she takes his little jingly-bobs in the palm of her hand and jiggles them a bit. Then she slaps his arse cheeks and, scratching among the hairs, starts pulling at his thingy again, until the cucumber, fully ripe, looks like someone who's trying to retch and can't quite manage it. The poor lovesick fool is beside himself with all these caresses and wouldn't trade his pleasure for that of a piglet being scratched; and when he sees himself being mounted by the woman he was about to mount, he'll melt like a man coming.

PIPPA: What am I hearing?

NANNA: Listen and learn how to sell your merchandise. By my faith, Pippa, if a woman climbing onto her lover does even a particle of what I'm about to tell you, she'll be able to charm money from his shin-bones more easily than dice and cards get it out of gamblers.

PIPPA: I believe you.

NANNA: Take it as read.

PIPPA: Do you want me to do all this no matter who I bed down with?

NANNA: Yes, do it.

PIPPA: How can I do it if he's on top of me?

NANNA: There's no shortage of ways to make him jump off!

PIPPA: Show me one.

NANNA: Here's one. While he's labouring the leather, start crying, act bashful, stop moving, and fall silent. If he asks you what's wrong, let out a groan as well; if you do that he'll have to stop and say: 'My dear, am I hurting you? Are you displeased at the pleasure I'm taking?' And you say: 'My dear old chap, I'd like…' But here stop short and he'll ask: 'What?' and you just moan. At last, through words and gestures, make it clear to him that you want to ride a little gallop on his stick.

PIPPA: Now suppose I'm where you say I should be.

NANNA: Imagine yourself doing as I say: arrange yourself with care, and once you're in a convenient position, throw your arms around his neck and kiss him ten times in a row. Then taking his pestle in hand, clasp it so hard that it goes wild, and, when it's all fired up, shove it into your hub, pushing yourself all the way onto him. Stop here and kiss him, and after a moment sigh excitedly and say: 'If I come, will you come too?' The stallion will answer in a lustful voice: 'Yes, my love.' So you start twisting around, as if his spike was the shaft and your little herb patch the wheel that revolves on it, and if he looks like he's about to come, hold back saying: 'Not yet, my dear', sticking your tongue in his mouth without letting his key slip out of your lock. Then push, wriggle, and drive, slow and firm; give him the cut and thrust, and touch all his keys like a true paladin. I'll have you using all those little manoeuvres that football players use while they've got the ball – weaving artfully, and pretending to run this way and that, they gain so much time that they foil their opponent and take the shot as they please.

PIPPA: You warn me to be decent, then you teach me shameless indecency.

NANNA: I'm not being inconsistent. I want you to be as much of a whore in bed as you are a lady elsewhere, so that the men who sleep with you can't imagine a caress you won't give them. And always be on the lookout so you can scratch them where it itches. Ha! Ha! Ha!

PIPPA: What are you laughing at?

NANNA: I'm laughing at the excuse they come up with when their tails don't stand up.

PIPPA: What excuse is that?

NANNA: They blame it on their excessive love, and well they may, because if they didn't use that excuse, they'd be more at a loss than a doctor whose patient, when asked if he's moved his bowels, says yes – he's no idea what to prescribe. He ends up as ashamed as an old man who, after climbing on top, can only satisfy us with doubloons and chit-chat.

PIPPA: That's just what I wanted to ask you: how I should manage when I'm under some drivelling farter who stinks from above and below, and how can I put up with being crushed by him lying on top of me all night. My cousin told me that some girl or other fainted away in that position.

NANNA: My dear, the sweet scent of money prevents the rotten stench of their breath and the foul smell of their feet from reaching your nose. And getting a slap is worse than bearing with the cesspit in the mouth of a man who'll pay in gold for your tolerance of his defects. Now pay close attention, I'm going to explain how to cope with all manner of musical *musicorum*, and how to handle their natural attributes. If you suffer them with patience, you'll be more the mistress of what they possess than I am yours and mine.

PIPPA: Tell me a bit about these old chaps.

NANNA: Well, here you are at supper with those lechers who've got goodwill and miserable legs. Now, Pippa, there is food in abundance, wine on demand, and gentlemanly chit-chat. Anyone who listened to them boast would say: 'These men must go at it like the clappers', and if their prowess in bed were anything like the results they achieve with pheasants and malmsey wine, they would cast Orlando himself into the shade.[3] Why, if they satisfied their women by screwing them as well as they satisfy them by providing good titbits to eat, then lucky girls! These boastful eager beavers, pinning their hopes on peppers, truffles, thistles and certain warm tinctures imported from France, take in more bellyfuls than peasants do harvesting grapes. And gulping down oysters without chewing, they expect to perform miracles. At dinners like this you can pretty much eat without ceremony.

PIPPA: Why?

NANNA: Because their pleasure is to spoonfeed you as you would a baby; and they're happier watching you eat as if you were starved, than a horse is at hearing the water-boy's whistle. What's more, old men are the enemies of formality.

PIPPA: So when I eat with them, I can do away with the self-restraint you talked about.

NANNA: By God's cross you've got it; if you keep on making progress like that, the others will be left like a priest without alms. Now I had almost forgotten to warn you not to clean your teeth with the napkin and rinse them with fresh water after dining with the old men (as you should do when you eat with the younger ones), since they could take offence, thinking to themselves: 'She's mocking our teeth, which hang shakily in our mouths, only stuck on with wax.'

PIPPA: But I'll want to clean them, out of spite.

NANNA: Nonsense.

PIPPA: All right then, I won't clean them.

NANNA: You can pick at them just as well with a sprig of rosemary on the sly.

PIPPA: Come on now, let's get on to sleeping with them.

NANNA: Ha! Ha! Ha! I can't help laughing, because they'll have to keep away from the toilet as I've said you should. Oh, what farts, what stenches they let loose! The bellows of a blacksmith don't blow that hard. And while they're contorting their snouts with the effort, forcing themselves to shit out twines, they'll have a bag of liquorice in one hand to soothe the cough that tortures them. Once they've taken off their doublets, they're really a joy to look at. In any case, remembering their youth as jackasses and she-asses do green vine stems, they get all excited, and hungrier than ever. And I could hardly recite all the simpering nonsense they reel off to cajole a girl as they hug her – their favourite treat is the kind of gibberish used by nurses with infants who don't know what's what. They'll put the sparrowhawk in your fist, suck on your tits, get astraddle, and twist and turn you this way and that. You keep moving around, tickling their armpits and sides, and when you feel their thingy coming to itself, grab it again and shake it so artfully that it raises its head bit by bit.

PIPPA: So even these old codgers' ones rise up proudly?

NANNA: Sometimes, but they come back down again just as quickly; and if you'd seen your father (God bless him), during his illness, trying to sit up in bed and quickly falling back, you could imagine one of these old pricks; they're like earthworms folding into themselves and pushing out again as they crawl along.

PIPPA: Mother, you've taught me what I have to do while I'm on top, and all the appropriate extras, but not how I should finish off.

NANNA: Don't say another word, because I know what you're getting at, and my heart swells so much with pride at seeing you at home in these affairs that I'm in raptures. Now, going back, you want me to tell you what good are all these saucy tricks you use when you're sitting on the 'fucker' (as we commonly say).

PIPPA: You've hit the nail on the head.

NANNA: Do you remember, Pippa, when Zoppino sang the tale of Campriano at the market?

PIPPA: I remember the Zoppino who made the whole world run to hear him when he sang.

NANNA: That's the fellow. Do you remember how you laughed, as you listened to him together with Luchina and Lucietta, when we were visiting my godfather Piero?

PIPPA: Yes, ma'am.

NANNA: Then you know that Zoppino sang about how Campriano stuck three pounds worth of change up his donkey's arse, and, riding him to Siena, sold him to two traders for a hundred ducats each, making them think he could shit coins.

PIPPA: Ha! Ha! Ha!

NANNA: So, anyway, he told the tale halfway and when he had drawn a nice big crowd, he changed the subject and before finishing the story he started touting a thousand other trifles.

PIPPA: I don't like that.

NANNA: Do you know, prop and stay of my old age, what will happen to you if you let me finish talking?

PIPPA: What?

NANNA: The same thing that happens when you watch a man dive under water while swimming – you always see him reappear where you were least expecting. I'm telling you that as you've brought him to ecstasy with your clever handling and he's about to spit the slug, stop suddenly and cry, 'I can't go on'. Then, even if he begs, just say, 'I can't'.

PIPPA: I'll also say, 'I won't'.

NANNA: Yes do, because it'll make him as desperate as a man who is parched by thirst from a burning fever and sees a bucket of fresh water, which, out of pity, his servant has just drawn from the well to give him, snatched right out of his hand. And when he sees you're about to dismount the saddle, he'll promise you all sorts of fine things – but don't be swayed. In the end, he'll dive for his purse, and let you have it all; and while pretending you don't want it, stretch out your hand to grab it, because saying 'I won't' and 'I can't', just at the right moment is the same recipe Zoppino used, leaving the merry crowd high and dry by cutting short his Campriano story.

PIPPA: And the job's done. Now, back to the old fellows.

NANNA: With an old fogey who sweats and pants more than a man with fear up his arse, and wears you out with his trying and failing, you need to play a little game. Rest your face on his breast and say, 'Who's your girl? Who's your flesh and blood?' and 'Who's your daughter? Daddy, darling Daddy, Daddikins, aren't I your little pet?' and tickle every pimple and wrinkle you find on his body. Sing him a lullaby, humming softly and treating him like someone in their second childhood. And he'll behave just like a child, I'm certain, calling you 'Mummy, sweet Mummy, Mummikins'. Whilst all this is happening, you'll be facing him directly and feeling for his purse under the pillow; if it's there, don't leave him a penny, and if it's not, get it there. You have to resort to these tricks, because these misers can quibble for four hours over a penny not spent for their pleasure; and if they promise you gowns or necklaces, don't leave their side until the gift is ordered. Then, with his fingers or whatever he wants to use, let him do it forwards, backwards, sideways – it really doesn't matter!

PIPPA: Don't worry.

NANNA: Now listen to this: these men are jealous types who fly into violent rages, throwing their hands about and cursing like beasts, but if they take a fancy to you, not only will you be showered with gifts, but you'll have a whale of a time, too. Why, I can just see him now, that old codger, staler than Noah's great-grandfather, with his breeches and brocaded doublet all worn away, wearing a plumed velvet cap, with metal-tipped laces and a gold medal with a diamond hammer, a sterling silver beard, arms and legs trembling, and a withered face, tottering about all day long outside your house, whistling, howling and snorting like a cat in January. And I'm about to piss in my drawers from giggling just thinking of a little trick that is out of this world.

PIPPA: Tell me it.

NANNA: Once a sly charlatan made an old man believe he had a special dye for his beard and hair, such a dark mulberry black that a devil would look white by comparison. But he

19

wanted to sell it so dear that it took several days of listening to his patter before the old man gave in. Finally, feeling that his leek-like head and straw-like beard were diminishing his reputation as a lover, he forked out twenty-five Venetian ducats for the charlatan, who, either to make fun of him or to cheat him, turned his hair and beard the brightest turquoise blue that ever was painted on the tail of a Barbary or Turkish horse; in the end he had to be shorn down to his hide. He was the talk of the town for a long time – in fact, people still laugh about it.

PIPPA: Ha! Ha! Ha! I can just see him, the old dodderer. If I get my claws into one of these, I'll make him my fool.

NANNA: You'll do quite the opposite – never make fun of him for any reason, and especially in the company of others, because old people should be revered; besides, you would be considered a vile and wicked woman to tease a man like that. I want you to make a show of loving him, bowing to every little word he utters, so that other old men will feel young again and fall in love with you. And if you must laugh at him, do it here between us.

PIPPA: I'll do it, if it's the right thing to do.

NANNA: Let's talk about the nobility.

PIPPA: Yes, let's.

NANNA: Suppose there's a nobleman asking for you; either I can send you to him or you can go by yourself, it doesn't matter. It's best to put on a good show, because they're accustomed to grand ladies, and get more pleasure from discussions and chit-chat than from anything else. So you have to know how to talk: answer to the point, don't ramble on, going from pillar to post, otherwise not just His Lordship, but even his servants will sneer at you behind your back. Don't sit there looking too gauche or too flirtatious, but carry yourself gracefully. And if there's playing or singing, keep your ears fixed on the music or song, praising the musicians and the singers, even if you don't enjoy it or don't understand it. And if there's a scholar there, approach him with a cheerful face, showing you appreciate him more – yes, even more – than the master of the house.

PIPPA: Why do that?

NANNA: Out of respect.

PIPPA: Oh, come on!

NANNA: Why, all you need is for one of those fellows to attack you in writing, and to have the gossip spread everywhere, with those slanderous things they're so good at saying about women. You'd be in a nice fix if they were to put your life in print, like some good-for-nothing did mine, as if there weren't worse whores than myself around. If all their goings-on were spread around, they'd blot out the very sun. And how they barked on my account! Those who reproach me for what I said about nuns, saying, 'She lies about everything', don't realise that I told Antonia just to make her laugh, not to create a scandal, as I could easily have done; but the world isn't what it used to be, and an experienced person can't live in it any longer.

PIPPA: Don't get worked up.

NANNA: Look, Pippa, I was a nun, and I left because I left, and if I'd wanted to tell Antonia how they get married, and call their monk 'my little friend', while the monk calls his nun 'my little friend', I could very well have done so. And just listing the sorts of things those gut-buckets say to their 'little friends' when they return from some place they've been preaching in, would be enough to stupefy the stigmata. I know very well what they do with the widows who give them shirts, handkerchiefs and dinners, and all about their affairs and entanglements. And what about that preacher, who, as he was fulminating from the pulpit like a dragon, consigning us all to hell, dropped the biretta he kept stuffed up his sleeve amongst the crowd that was listening like a bunch of dumbfounded snotnoses. Everybody saw the hidden embroidery – in the centre of it, on the inside, there was a heart of flesh-coloured satin burning in a fire made of red silk, and around the edges in black letters was written,

> *Love requires faith – the ass a cudgel.*

The crowd, roaring with laughter, kept it as a relic. And as for the icons of St Nafissa and Masetto da Lamporecchio,[4] there's no truth in them at all; I'm absolutely certain that in their place, hanging from the walls, there are hair shirts, scourges with spikes, sharp-toothed combs, leather-strapped sandals, herb roots that testify to the fasting they don't observe, wooden bowls used to ration out water to those who abstain, dead men's skulls for contemplating death, shackles, ropes, manacles, whips – things that frighten those who look at them and not those who sin, nor those who hung them there.

PIPPA: Are there really so many stories?

NANNA: There are even more I can't remember. But what would any of those ignoramuses, those toffee-noses, have said if I had made public how the mistress of novices recognises whenever Sister Crescenzia or Sister Gaudenzia is on heat? You, gossips, scum of the earth! May you all be flogged for carping at the speech of someone who could be your teacher!

PIPPA: Why, aren't people allowed to speak as they wish?

NANNA: Let the fools ramble away – all they do is laugh at those who talk in their native dialect, while they mince their expressions as one minces chicory. I beg you, my dear, not to give up the speech your mother taught you, leaving the 'ergos' and 'anons' to the miladies. And let them have their way when, using some new or refined term, they say, 'Go, that the Heavens may be propitious and the hours propinquinous', and scoff at those who speak plainly, saying 'hurry up', 'in a bit', 'just now', 'puff', 'oy', 'yell', 'shambles', 'halfwit', 'sloosh', 'croak', 'clear as mud', and a hundred thousand other words without frills.

PIPPA: The crows!

NANNA: Well said! – they want us to say 'forthwith' instead of 'quickly', 'moistful' instead of 'wet', and if you ask them why they'll answer, 'Because "take" and "fetch" are against the rules'; it's become dangerous to open your mouth these days. But I'm still myself, and I speak as I please, not with my cheeks puffed out, spitting out salamonics. I walk with my own feet, not a crane's, and I say the words just as they come; I don't fork them out of my mouth. They're just words, not confectionaries, and when I talk I look like a woman, not a magpie. So Nanna is Nanna, and the rabble that goes about shitting et ceteras, looking for hairs to split, don't have enough credit to cover their backsides. In the end, those who carp about everything without ever stirring their own arses will never get their names out of the taverns, while mine's been trotted all the way to Turkey. So, you ninnies, I intend to frame and weave my cloth in my own way, since I know where to find the yarn to fill the rows, and I've plenty of reels to darn and patch my runs and cuts with.

PIPPA: Those washed-up wretches are playing with fire; they're asking to get the finger from us one of these days, in front of everybody, if they keep on muttering about our way of talking.

NANNA: You can be sure of it. And let me tell you this: a fortune-teller, a witch, a hag who teaches parrots how to twitter, asked me the other day what 'chatting up', 'mucking around', 'pissed off', 'fancy', 'flabbergasted', 'slick', and 'whopper' meant, and as I was spelling them out for her, she was writing them all down. Now she parades them around as if they were her own stuff. But I live a simple life and I don't give a hoot – I don't care if 'zilch' is commoner than 'nought'.

PIPPA: Don't dwell on those fusspots any longer, because my brain is getting muddled and I might forget the things that really matter.

NANNA: You're right – the anger I feel for those purebreds who rack their brains to make salads and spicy sauces out of underfed words, and who, with the obstinacy of ticks and crab-lice, want to triumph at all costs, has caused me to lose my way. But I remember I was telling you how you must flatter the scholars who you'll find, more often than not, at noblemen's tables.

PIPPA: That's just what you were saying.

NANNA: Flatter them, talk to them, and to show you appreciate talent, ask them for a sonnet, a *strambotto*, a *capitolo* – nonsense like that. And when they offer you one, kiss them and thank them as if you'd just been given jewels. And when they come knocking at your door, always let them in, because they're perfectly discreet and if they see you're occupied, they'll leave without further ado, courting you only when you're free.

PIPPA: And if I just didn't feel like opening the door to them, what would happen?

NANNA: You'd be lashed by the cruellest abuse that ever was heard – such a temperament they have, going to war at every phase of the moon – and they'd be quite indignant at what you'd done, so watch yourself. And – as it is common practice for women to ramble on all the time – before I get back to the nobleman you'll be sleeping with, I want to tell you a nice little trick that slipped my mind as I was talking about the old men.

PIPPA: It must be a good one, since you're retracing your steps to tell me.

NANNA: Ha! Ha! I want you, Pippa, to pick up five of those sweets that are scattered all over the table after the cloth is removed and, tossing them in the air, say, 'If they make a lovely cross, my dear sweet old man loves only me; if the cross is crooked, he adores so-and-so.' If it comes out right, Pippa, raise your hands to the heavens and then, stretching your arms out wide, wrap yourself around him, giving him a kiss with as many endearments as you can think of; you'll see him drop to the floor, like someone dying of heat when he feels a breath of fresh air. If the cross happens to turn out badly, let a couple of little tears escape, if you can, accompanied by a few stealthy sighs. And then get up from your chair and go to the fireside, making a show of stirring it with the tongs to let off steam. When he sees this, the cretinous ox will hurl himself at you, dotingly swearing, by his body and blood, that he does love you. Then you flounce off to the bedroom and put your feet up for a while before making it up with him.

PIPPA: I'll do as you say, Mummy.

NANNA: I have every faith, my dear. So here you are with the nobleman, a man who brags about his lovers, saying: 'Lady Such-and-Such, Madame So-and-So, the Duchess, and the Queen' – and whatever other shit he'll come out with – 'did me this service, and this other lady another,' and you should congratulate him on his 'servicings', and be surprised that all the beauties of Tunis are not converting so they can have him on top of them. And while he goes on about the feats he performed during the siege of Florence and the sack of Rome, sidle up to the man nearest you, remarking, so the good-for-nothing hears you, 'Oh, what a handsome man! His beauty puts me all out of sorts.' He'll pretend not to hear, but will start peacocking around. And bear in mind that if you don't resort to the kind of tricks that scraping sycophants use with the monsignors, valuing villainy above hierarchy, you'll make an enemy of them.

PIPPA: I've got it.

NANNA: Flattery and deceit are the darlings of great men, as they say, and so with these men spread the butter on thick, if you want to get something out of them, otherwise you'll come home to me with a full belly and an empty purse. And if it weren't for the fact that their friendship gives more honour than it does profit, I'd teach you to avoid them, because they want to be the only ones at the banquet; and since they are lords, they think you shouldn't give yourself to anyone else. And if you don't come to them or open up, they'd think no more of sending their footmen to cause trouble at your door, in your street, at your windows and with the maid, than they would of spitting on the ground. They're like those mutts that come upon a pack of whelps mounting a little bitch, and after tearing them away with growls and bites, hog her themselves. And there's no doubt that this sort of behaviour sends anyone afraid to compete with them running, and it's perfect for those women who care more for the smoke than the roast.

PIPPA: God help me with these lords.

NANNA: But I want to give you a little tip, so that even if the villains drop dead, it'll cost them. When His Highness begins undressing for bed, take his cap and put it on your head, then put on his gown and take a couple of little turns around the room. As soon as the gentleman sees you transformed from a woman into a man, he'll jump on you like hunger on hot bread, and unable to wait until you get into bed, he'll want you with your head resting against the wall or a linen chest. The point is that you should let yourself be drawn and quartered rather than give in to him, unless he gives you his cap and gown, so that next time you can go to him dressed in the clothes that lords like best.

PIPPA: I get the picture.

NANNA: But, above all, study deceit and flattery as I've told you, because these are the frills that help you to earn a living. Men want to be duped; and while they realise they're being conned and that, when you've left their side, you'll mock them and brag about it even to your maids, they still prefer fake caresses to real ones without the sweet talk. Never give short measure of kisses, glances, smiles, and chit-chat; hold his hand at all times, and every now and then nip at his lips all of a sudden with your teeth, so that he gives that sweet 'Aaah!' that men let out when they feel a pang of bliss. The cornerstone of a whore's art is knowing how to feed gammon to the gullible.

PIPPA: I get it loud and clear.

NANNA: I'm thinking…

PIPPA: What?

NANNA: ...that while I'm teaching you all the ways to get where I want you, I'm also guiding those who will have dealings with you, since, knowing what I tell you, you can be sure that they'll also know when you're using your wiles. So my instruction is like one of those paintings that looks down from all angles at whoever looks at it.

PIPPA: Who do you think would make it known?

NANNA: This room, that bed over there, the chairs we're sitting in, that little window there, and this fly that wants to nibble at my nose – the devil take it! – Flies may be persistent, but those who are jealous are even more annoying; they become a nuisance even to themselves, with all their candlelight scheming, trying to keep an eye on a woman who can't be kept in check when she decides to cheat them. A beast of that colour needs careful management; sooner give him horns than explanations. So listen: you're the lover of one man, and he'll be jealous of another man who could be quite helpful to you – not as helpful as the first man, but so helpful that it would be very damaging to lose him. The first man will order you not to open your door to him, not to speak to him or accept anything from him. Here you need to use the most diabolical oaths, brazen faces, head-shaking, raised voices, and other gestures that demonstrate your astonishment at the man who thinks you would exchange him for that sheep. And saying, 'God forbid you think I would throw myself away on that donkey-faced knucklehead,' demand yourself that he have you watched, say you'll pay for the spies, and if he locks you up, just put up with it. If his suspicions still don't diminish, don't waste your time. Use what you have wheedled out of him and spend it on comforts for the poor exile; smuggle him into the house when the jealous man goes out, either as the wood is being unloaded or as the bread is taken to the bakehouse. If his frenzy gets worse, tell your lover to come to you at night and hide him in the maid's room, where you must be sure to set a chamber pot so you can do your business. And in the evening deliberately eat something to make your bowels move, or pretend to have pains in your side and run off groaning. Hurry off to the other man, who, waiting for you, fife in hand, will fire off two shots with a single load. The sweet ecstasy tickling you all over will make you cry, 'Oh God!' and 'I'm dying!' with more aching passion than childbirth. When you've done the job, go back to the first man, relieved of any discomfort. That's the recipe for having your cake and eating it, as Cardinal Armellini's major-domo used to say.[5]

PIPPA: I'll do it.

NANNA: If this lunatic happens to smell a rat, raise your hand in denial and, with a straight face, keep saying, 'It's not true!' If he gets furious, humble yourself and say, 'So you take me for one of those women, eh? And if people gossip, can I stop their tongues? If I had wanted other men, I wouldn't have chosen you and I wouldn't have become a nun for the sake of your love.' And while you clamour on like that, get as close to him as you can; and if a few slaps get thrown, be patient, for he'll soon be paying for the doctors and the medicines; and all the coaxing you have to do to sweeten him up, he'll be doing himself to console you; and all the 'Forgive me's and 'I was wrong to believe it's will motivate you to be good and loving towards him. If you were to confess your sin or try to take revenge for those four slaps that come and go, you could either lose him or anger him so much that it would end badly for you. It's no lie that the effort lies in keeping lovers, not in acquiring them.

PIPPA: No doubt about it.

NANNA: Moving on, you'll also come across men who aren't jealous but can still be in love, despite those who insist there is no love without jealousy. For a man carved from this timber, there's a tincture, which, in just one or two sips, can rouse an entire whorehouse to fits of jealousy.

PIPPA: What tincture is that?

NANNA: Get someone you can trust to write you a little letter, like this one I learnt by heart:

Madam,
I cannot wish you health at the beginning of this letter, because there is no health in me; I can recover it only if your pity will allow me to tell you, in that place that is most convenient for you, what I dare not confide in writing or by messenger. And so I implore by your divine beauty, that Nature, with God's consent, has borrowed from the angels to bestow on you, to be allowed to speak: for I have things to say that shall make you happy, and the more so, the sooner I obtain the audience I beg for on bended knee. And so I await a reply that savours of the grace that radiates from your lovely countenance. And should you refuse to grant it to me, as you refused the pearls I sent you, not as a gift but as a sign of goodwill, etc., I shall escape from my woes by steel or rope or poison.

I kiss Your gracious Ladyship's hand –

with the address and signature, which, in a situation like this, the person writing will know how to do.

PIPPA: What should I do with it once it's written?

NANNA: Fold it carefully and slip it into a glove, then carelessly drop it somewhere, so that the jealousy, which before filled only his socks, will grow so much it fills his lungs. As soon as the wretch picks up the glove, he'll feel the letter, and as soon as he's felt it, he'll steal it, and withdraw into a little corner, hiding from everyone else. As he begins to read, he'll frown, and when he gets to the part about the rejected pearls, he'll hiss like a viper, his courage dropping to his boots, and the bile rising in his throat. I'm telling you, the devil gets into a man when he comes across a rival. And words can't describe the fever that shakes a man who, while thinking he was without a companion at the meat block, sees someone slip past who jeopardises the entire piece of flesh. Having read and reread the forged note, he'll put it back where he found it, that is, inside the glove. All the while you will be spying on him through a chink or keyhole, and when you spot the right moment protest loudly to your maid: 'Where's my glove, you idiot? Where is it, you scatterbrain?' The lovelorn fellow will come into view, and you shriek even louder, saying: 'You silly bitch, you'll be the cause of some scandal, and perhaps even my ruin. If that letter falls into his hands I'll never be able to persuade him that I wanted to show it to him and tell him about the man who's been writing me all that rubbish. God knows not even pearls or ducats would have the power to make me another man's mistress!' When he hears this, the dupe will curb his anger and, after thinking a little to himself, will call you and say: 'Here it is, stop yelling. I have absolute faith in you. I've read it all, and you shan't lack for pearls. And I beg you not to tell me the name of the man who's been making you these magnificent offers, because perhaps, perhaps...' And here, as he falls silent, you will say: 'I never wanted to tell you how I've been pestered by messengers and... but that's enough. I'm yours and I want to be yours, and when I am dead I shall still be entirely yours.'

PIPPA: Tell me what this plot will achieve.

NANNA: It'll mean that, after finding the letter, the man will have no peace of mind left. In fact, he'll believe that every man he sees on your street is either the one who sent it to you or his goon, and, so as not to give you reason to accept any offers, he'll start being more generous. Now, let's get on to these Mantuans (not the ones from Ferrara), who, as soon as they have secured a room at a lodge, go flirting about as if the frills and furbelows that spoil their capes and doublets gave them the privilege of a 'free dispensation', as they say at the Vatican. Pippa, if you manage to get your claws into any of these upstarts, slyly find out when they're leaving, calculating the time by the rings, medallions, necklaces, underwear and other odds and ends that you see on them, because you can't rely on their money, and since there's little chance of their ever coming back, you needn't worry whether they praise or insult you.

PIPPA: It shall be done, but how do you know about their money?

NANNA: I know that they never bring enough of it to get them back home. And if you get messed up with them, strip them of all those knick-knacks, otherwise you'll be left with your hands full of their slimy flattery.

PIPPA: If they try that on me, I'll give them what for.

NANNA: And if you happen to sleep with one of them, take a good look at his belongings, whether it be a shirt or a nightcap; and in the morning, before he gets up, call for the pedlar with her mountains of tat. Once you've compared all her stuff to the Mantuan's rags, have them taken away or throw them on the floor; and show your temper with that cuckoo, grumbling so much that he'll offer you his own things. And if he doesn't, coax him back to bed and clean him out by fraud or force.

PIPPA: When you were young did you do all the things you're telling me to do?

NANNA: It was different in my day, and I did what I could, as you'll hear if you have someone read you the story of my life published by that Mr A-plague-on-him. I omit his name as he's very touchy and he could do worse to me than those beastly lovers of yours will do to you if you don't learn how to keep them on side. You might say: 'I won't get caught up with people like that', but that's not how it works.

PIPPA: Why not?

NANNA: Because, even with your kind of savvy, you can't avoid having some of them buzz around you. So let them rave whenever they lose their temper, and shut your ears to the 'whore, pig, slut', which they'll utter in a single breath; and although they try to crush the world with the words they drown in spittle, spattering the face of anyone nearby, nothing more will come of it. And in less time than it takes to say two Credos, they will calm down again, asking your forgiveness, giving you gifts, and worming their way back into your heart. I used to enjoy hanging around these men, because they get angry at nothing and calm down at nothing; their anger is like an overcast sky in July: despite the thunder and lightning, after twenty-five drops have fallen, out comes the sun again. So your patience will make you rich.

PIPPA: Let's be patient, then. What will come of it?

NANNA: They'll chase you until they die. Now, here you are with a shrewd one, a two-faced old fox, who weighs all your comings and goings, and disputes every little word, prodding his companion with his foot and twisting his mug, giving a little wink, as if to say: 'She wants to try it on with me, eh?' Keep control of yourself; never get upset – in fact always play the naive fool. Don't question him and don't argue with him. If he talks to you, talk to him, if he kisses you, kiss him, and if he gives you something, take it. And use such cunning arts on him that he can never catch you doing the business. In fact, behave in such a way that he'll tell himself you're the best thing since sliced bread; but don't let him weed your garden unless he pays for the ground in which he wants to sow his seed; and when he tries to baffle you with his mischief, muster up all your cunning to make him believe that there's nothing suspect about you. So then the great nitpicker will be forced to entrust you with his untrusting trust; and caught between a rock and a hard place, he'll be yours while you won't be his unless you want to be.

PIPPA: I'm surprised, Mother, that you don't run a school to teach people all these sorts of tricks.

NANNA: I have qualities in me that would befit an empress; I'm not haughty, though I was in the past, God forgive me. But let's not waste time: learn how to show your temper and then how to make peace with your admirers as I am teaching you; and don't think it too long a lesson, that I mean you to have at the tip of your tongue, because whoredom has such a genius for invention that, even without a teacher, you can learn more than you could imagine in eight days. So just think how much further you'll go, having Nanna as your guide.

PIPPA: If you say so.

NANNA: That's how it'll be, don't worry. Lose your temper gracefully, Pippa. Do it in a certain way so everyone will think you're in the right. If your lover promises you the moon and the stars, wait patiently for a day or two for him to keep his promise, without breathing a word. By the middle of the third day, give him a little hint and he'll say: 'Don't you worry, you'll see and that's that.' Look cheery and talk about the man in the moon, the Pope who never croaks, the Emperor who performs miracles, *Orlando Furioso*, and '*The Prices of Venetian Courtesans*'[6] (which I ought to have mentioned earlier). Then let your chin drop onto your breast and suddenly fall silent, brooding for a while. And getting up, say with a faint voice: 'I don't believe it.' I can just see that gift-grudger saying: 'What's up now?'; then you say to him: 'Where were you last night?', and without waiting for his reply, run off to your room and lock yourself in. And if he knocks at the door, let him knock; if he barks, let him bark, because if I were you, I would always stand up to him, and swear you were told that he only comes to you to sate the lust he has for some other woman. And I'll bet that he'll set off downstairs, cursing and denying, and when he comes back in a while – or that very moment, or the next day – tell him you're busy or that you have company.

PIPPA: Yes, of course – peace will be made when he doubles the promise.

NANNA: Now I'm certain you'll make your own way and approach life differently to the way I did. Listen carefully: choose your own style of annoyance, I mean show your temper just when the bantering is at its best and slouch over with your cheek propped in your hand.

PIPPA: Why?

NANNA: So this man, who can't live without you, will come to you saying: 'What are these whims of yours? Do you feel sick? Do you need something? Tell me.' And he'll be extra polite to calm you down. And you answer: 'Just leave me alone, for God's sake; go on, bugger off – I mean it – are you, are you looking for trouble?' Be as rude as possible to show you don't think much of him. Do this even when he tries tickling you to make you laugh, and don't let a single smile escape you unless he gives you something; and when he does, be nice to him, since it's a well-known fact that even children who throw tantrums calm down when they're given toys.

PIPPA: This is child's play; I want you to tell me how I can make it up if, say, I've cheated on someone, or if they've cheated on me.

NANNA: I'll tell you. If you're the one who's been unfaithful, as must indubitably be the case, drop your shoulders and speak honestly, telling everyone: 'I've acted like a child, a foolish and careless woman; the devil blinded me, I don't deserve forgiveness, and if God spares me this once, never, never again will I break His commandments.' And then, opening the floodgates, cry more than you would if I were to turn up my toes – may God preserve me and take whoever wishes harm on us.

PIPPA: Amen.

NANNA: The squawking and crying you do will be reported to him on the gallop, because a man like that will always keep his spies on you, and whoever relates the news, adding on a little something of his own, will make him change his mind. And even though he swears he would sooner eat his own hands from hunger than speak to you again, and that he would rather let his enemies lead him to the slaughter-house, along with other vulgar oaths that drop through the teeth of those who get carried away with anger, nothing will come of it. Nor will he go to hell for his blasphemies, since the Good Lord God does not count the perjury of lovers, who can't be held to account while they rave in the heat of passion. And even though he's been stubborn since he was in swaddling-clothes, write him a sermon of a letter, then go and visit him at home and act like you want to break down his door. If he won't open up, start cursing outrageously, and if all this doesn't work pretend you're going to hang yourself, though make sure your play-acting doesn't become reality, causing you a mishap like what's-his-name in Modena.

PIPPA: Oh! If I ever hang myself, either in jest or in earnest, then string me up!

NANNA: Ha! Ha! Ha! Here's how you can unravel the knot. Search your house, in the chests and in every nook and cranny, and bundle up his shirts, his stockings and all his stuff, even down to a pair of tired old slippers, ancient gloves, a nightcap – any old rubbish – and any bracelets or rings he's given you, and send them all back to him.

PIPPA: I'm not going to do that.

NANNA: You'll do as I say, because seeing the presents he's given his mistress returned is the last straw for someone fading through the tortures of love; it makes it quite clear how much regard she has for him and his things. Misery will send him mad – as mad as mad can be – and without further hesitation he'll gather up the goods and send them straight back to you.

PIPPA: And what if he's a miser?

NANNA: Misers don't give anything away or leave anything of value behind. Take a chance, do what I advise, and if you don't end up consummating the peace, you can call me a fool. There are some women who plant themselves out-stretched on the bed, and as long as they're considered the best, think they've managed brilliantly if they can sell their flesh by the pound to the highest bidder. And it's just flesh, not goods sold at auction. Poor wretches, they don't realise they're going to end up where they were destined from the start, and all along – in hospitals and on bridges, where, frenchified, shattered and lonely, they'll make anyone who can bear to look at them retch with disgust. And let me tell you, my dear, that all the treasure found by those scrounging Spaniards in the New World would not compensate a whore, no matter how ugly and unlucky she might be. And whoever really takes into account how they live would be committing a mortal sin if he didn't acknowledge it. And to prove I'm speaking from the mouth of truth[7], take, for instance, a whore who is obligated to this or that man. She never has an hour's rest, whether she goes out or stays in, at the table or in bed. When she is sleepy, she can't sleep, in fact she has to stay awake to caress some mangy mut, or dung-breathed punter, or some brick shit-house who'll trample all over her; and if she baulks, then straight away he'll start whingeing: 'You don't deserve me, you're not worthy of me; if I were such-and-such a villain or scoundrel, you'd be wide awake.' If she's at table, every molehill looks like a mountain to him and if she gives a titbit to someone else, he grumbles and fumes with rage, chewing on his bread and his miserable jealousy. If she leaves, then he's in a fury; and saying to himself: 'I smell a rat', he'll sulk with her and go shouting from the rooftops the betrayal he thinks she's done him; and, bearing a grudge for some man or other, he won't rest. If she stays, and has that funny feeling that often makes people melancholic without really being melancholy, and can't put on her usual face, his suspicions rise up again: 'It's all perfectly clear.

I disgust you. I know very well where you're aching, very well indeed. Well, fine, you'll have plenty of men and I'll have plenty of women for my money – whores are ten a penny.' But still it would be a bed of roses if it weren't for that infamous infamy whose stench reaches down into the abyss and up into Heaven itself; we are pushed and shoved in every way, by day and by night; and any whore who doesn't consent to every obscene act imaginable will die of hunger. One likes his meat rare and another likes it well done, and they come up with the 'horizontal shuffle', 'legs in the air', 'side-saddle', the 'crane', the 'tortoise', the 'church steeple', the 'relay', the 'grazing sheep' and other postures stranger than the gestures of a mime. Even I, who can say 'been there, done that', am almost ashamed to list them. In short, nowadays they take apart any woman they want, so learn how to live, Pippa, and know how to survive, or I'll see you in hell.

PIPPA: Then it's true that there's more to being a whore than lifting one's skirts and saying: 'Come, I'm coming', as you said; and it's not about being a pretty face. You're an oracle.

NANNA: When a man spends ten ducats for all the pleasure he can get with a young girl, they say he's been as good as mugged; and if someone ends up in a shroud, the people are shocked and go around gossiping about how it must have been that deceiving bitch that ruined that nice lad. But when men gamble their very bones, renouncing their baptism and faith, then they're praised – the bastards. Let me finish telling you what I promised and then I'll spend all tomorrow going through the catalogue of thieving men; and I'll make you cry with tales of the cruelties and betrayals that the Turks, Moors, and Jews carry out on us poor women. And there's no poison, dagger, fire or flame that can revenge us. As for me, I have a couple of them hanging over me, still only partially paid off.

PIPPA: Don't get upset.

NANNA: How can I help feeling angry at those scoundrels? You'll hear how they take back what they give and how brave they are when they cut our faces and reward us with a 'thirty-one'[8]. Now, what I'm about to tell you about the prattle, manners and methods you must adopt at parties is no mean piece of advice – this is actually the key to the whole game.

PIPPA: That's what I'm after.

NANNA: And that's what you'll get. The ability to entertain men with that particular type of chit-chat they always enjoy is the very icing on the cake – *and* the cherry on top; and it's a sweet novelty, when you find yourself in the company of different sorts of people, to satisfy them all with interesting gossip. A few witty remarks and subtle hints for anyone who shows an interest are especially good; and, since people's ways are more varied than their characters, study, observe, anticipate, consider, reflect, discriminate and get inside everyone's head. Here you have a Spaniard, spruced up and perfumed, as delicate as the bottom of a china cup, which breaks as soon as you touch it, his sword at his side, all airs, as his footman behind him cries: 'Long leeve de Empress!', and all his other fripperies around him. You say to him: 'I don't deserve that so great a knight should pay me such honours. I pray that Your Lordship replace his hat; I shall not listen until it is replaced.' And if the 'Your Highness's he'll dizzy you with and the kisses he'll slurp onto your hands had the magic to make you rich, then what with that and all his other gallantries, you'd be wealthier than the heir of Croesus.

PIPPA: There's nothing to be gained with those men, I'm sure.

NANNA: All you have to do is give it back tit for tat, and pay them in hot air for those moans they so gutfully produce. Bow to their bows, kissing their glove, not just their hand, and if you don't want them to pay you with the tale of the conquest of Milan, get rid of them as soon as possible.

PIPPA: I will.

NANNA: Be sure to. Now, there's a Frenchman. Open your door at once, open it up in a flash; and while he cheerfully cuddles and French-kisses you, order up the wine. With men of this nation you can forget the usual attitude of whores, who wouldn't hand you a glass of water if they saw you dying; and after a couple of slices of bread, start cosying up to him. Without too much preamble, agree to sleep with him, politely sending the others away. He'll fill your kitchen full of so much food, it'll look like Carnival-time. And what else? He'll escape your claws in just his nightshirt, because these boozers are better at spending than earning, and better at forgetting themselves than remembering any injury, so they won't care a straw whether you rob them or not.

PIPPA: Honest Frenchmen, God bless you all!

NANNA: And just remember that they give you diamonds, while the Spaniards give you hearts. Now, the Germans are cut from a different mould and it's worth having designs on them. I'm talking about the merchants who get so caught up in their love affairs, not like they do with wine – I've actually known some very well-mannered ones – but like they do in their Lutheran devotions; and they'll give you ducats aplenty if you know how to get on the right side of them and don't spread it around that they are your lovers or boast about what they do or say to you. Strip them in secret – they will let themselves be stripped.

PIPPA: That's a good one to remember.

NANNA: By nature they're stern, bitter and beastly; and when they get something into their heads, God alone can drive it out, so butter them up with the sweetness of your understanding.

PIPPA: And what else should I do?

NANNA: There's something I want to suggest, but I don't dare.

PIPPA: What?

NANNA: Nothing.

PIPPA: Tell me, I want to know.

NANNA: I'm not going to – I'd be blamed and condemned.

PIPPA: Then why did you put the thought in my head?

NANNA: OK, I'll tell you, devil take it. If you can hang around with the Jews, then go ahead, but be careful; find an excuse, like you want to buy capes, bedroom accessories, or those sort of knick-knacks, and you'll see that straight away some man will slap on the counter a deposit of all his usuries and swindlings, even adding on interest. And if they stink like dogs, let them stink.

PIPPA: Is that all you wanted to tell me?

NANNA: What can I say? The fetid smell that hangs around them had me worried about telling you. But you know how it is: the extravagant earnings of those who go to sea can be put down to the dangers of the Catalan pirate ships, of drowning, of falling into the hands of Redbeard's Turks, of shipwrecks, eating stale, wormy bread, drinking watered-down vinegar, and other discomforts I've heard tell of; and if seafarers can bear the wind and the rain and all the other hardships in order to peddle their goods, then why should a courtesan scoff at the stench of a Jew?

PIPPA: You come out with some lovely similes. But if I get mixed up with them, what will my lovers say?

NANNA: What can they say if they don't know?

PIPPA: Why wouldn't they know?

NANNA: You won't tell them, will you? And the Jew will keep as quiet as a thief, for fear of having his bones broken.

PIPPA: I get it.

NANNA: Now I see a Florentine in your room with his nattering. Cover him with caresses, because Florentines away from Florence are like people with full bladders who don't dare piss out of respect for the place they're in. Yet once they're out of there, they'd fill a lake with the urine that gushes from their pikes. What I mean is that they are more open-handed elsewhere than they are tight-fisted at home; added to which they are clever, courteous, refined, witty and amusing; and even if they fed you on nothing more than their charming talk, you'd be quite content, wouldn't you?

PIPPA: Not me.

NANNA: It's just a figure of speech: suffice it to say they spend as much as they can, give papal banquets and feasts with a special flair that the others don't have, and, besides, everyone likes their language.

PIPPA: Now tell me a bit about the Venetians.

NANNA: I'm not going to tell you, because if I said everything they deserve to have said about them, people would tell me: 'Love has blinded you.' But in fact it hasn't blinded me at all, for they are gods and masters of everything, and the most beautiful youths, the most beautiful men, and the most beautiful old boys in the world. And when you take all those others out of their pompous robes, they look like wax puppets in comparison; and although the Venetians are proud – with good reason – they are goodness personified. Even though they count their pennies, when it comes to us they spend royally, and whoever knows how to get on their

43

right side will be content. It's all a farce, apart from those coffers they have crammed full of ducats, and come hell or high water, you know they won't just give you a pittance.

PIPPA: God bless them!

NANNA: Bless them He will.

PIPPA: But now I come to think of it, tell me why the lady who came back from there the other day couldn't bear it, and according to what my godmother said, she returned here with twenty pairs of strongboxes full of stones.

NANNA: I'll tell you. The Venetians have their own peculiar tastes and they want soft firm arses, tits and flesh, between fifteen or sixteen and twenty years old, and no Petrarchan subtleties. And so, my dear, put aside your courtesan manners and give them what they want, if you want them to throw shimmering gold at you and not misty words. And as for myself, if I were a man, I'd want to bed down with a woman who had a honeyed tongue and not a learned one; and I would feel happier holding a beautiful woman in my arms than the works of Messer Dante himself. And it seems a different tune to me that's played by a daring hand gently plucking at a bosom like a lute, settling just on the nipple, not too inverted nor too prominent. And the sound of a hand slapping the sanctum of the buttocks seems to me like a different melody to the music made by the fife players at the Castel Sant'Angelo when the cardinals visit the Vatican, dressed in those cowls that make them look like owls in a tree trunk. And I can just see this same hand leaving its strumming and finding its way home down the bodice, which, as it breathes in and sighs out, rises and falls as a painting would if it were alive.

PIPPA: Oh, you're such a painter with words, I'm getting excited just listening to you. It felt like the hand you were describing was touching my breasts and… no, I can't say it.

NANNA: I could see you were excited just by your face: it changed completely, then you went red, as I made you see unseen things. And now, jumping from Florence to Siena, I'd have to say that those barmy Sienese are the sweetest of madmen – though they've got worse in recent years, so they say – and of all the men I've had dealings with, I reckon they're the best. They have something of the Florentine about them, as far as their courtesy and virtues go, though they're not as shrewd or as stingy. A woman who knows how to hoodwink them will be able to shear them right down to the hide – they're actually just dupes with honourable and pleasant manners.

PIPPA: Then they're just right for me.

NANNA: Of course they are. Now onwards to Naples.

PIPPA: Don't say another word – just thinking about them gives me heart failure.

NANNA: Now, *hearken, milady, for your death's life.* The Neapolitans are there to keep you from dozing off, or to give you a good feed once a month, maybe, when you're in the mood for it, or when you're on your own or with someone of no importance. I can tell you their bragging reaches sky-level: bring up the subject of horses, and they have the best ones from Spain; clothes, and they have two or three wardrobefuls; they have piles of money, and all the beauties of the realm are dying to be with them. And if you drop a handkerchief or a glove, they'll pick it up with the loveliest turns of phrase ever to be heard at the Court of Capua – yes indeed.

PIPPA: How funny!

NANNA: I used to torment a brute named Giovanni Agnese, by imitating his speech – even the hangman couldn't imitate his deeds; he was the scum of the villainy of villains – and I used to have a Genoese man in stitches over him; one day I turned to him and said: 'Oh Genoese – so hard to please: you know how to buy your meat without getting any of the gristle; what can we scrape together to give you?' And so it is, for they can carve out the finest from the fine, and the sharpest from the sharp; and they know how to manage their business – they stir the stew with skill and they wouldn't give you a drop extra. And yet I can't begin to tell you how lavish they can be, how fond of Spanishified Neapolitan graces, and how respectful – making the little something they give you taste like sugar, they never let you go short of the necessary. Give these fellows their money's worth, measuring out your wares as they measure out theirs. And don't be put off by their throaty, nasal, sobbing talk; take it as it comes.

PIPPA: Men from Bergamo are more attractive than their language, too.

NANNA: You're right, some of them are sweet and adorable. But let's get onto those Romans – save yourself from my clobbering, Rienzo![9] My dear, if you enjoy living on bread and cheese, with a salad of swords and pikes, seasoned with the feats their great-grandfathers performed against the sheriff, then by all means hang around with them. But on the day of the sack[10] they shat themselves (pardon my French) and that's why Pope Clement hasn't looked at them since.

PIPPA: Don't forget Bologna. If for nothing else, then for the love of the Count and the Knight who are now part of the family.

NANNA: Forget them? Why, what would whores' rooms be like without the shadow of their long, overgrown shafts? They were only –

– as the poem goes. Of love, not arms, I sing! Brother Mariano said he'd never seen such plump-faced or well-dressed fools, according to a fine capon of his of about twenty. 'So, Pippa, you must fuss over them, as they'll be your Court hangers-on, and take pleasure in their frivolous and cloying gabble. And having them around isn't entirely without its uses, though it would be even better if they enjoyed the she-goat the way they do the billy! As for the rest of the Lombards, those jackasses and peacocks, handle them like a good whore, wheedling out as much as you can as quick as you can. Call them by the title of 'knight' or 'count' – 'Yes sir, no sir' is what they like best. With these men a little swindling won't spoil the soup, and it's quite respectable to con them and then boast about it, because they cheat poor courtesans, too, and then go bragging about it in all the taverns they stay in. And now, so you'll understand what it's like to cheat without cheating, I want to tell you a couple of stories I haven't told that blabbermouth Antonia. In fact, I've kept them hidden in my bosom for a rainy day.

PIPPA: Oh! Let me hear them.

NANNA: The first trick is the lowest of the low, and the second is the highest of the high. Let's start with the little one: I had a girl who died on me at thirteen, round and plump, very pretty, clever, crafty, naughty as they come, and, God knows, a real chatterbox – such a little fox, such a double-dealer as would make you run a mile. I taught her what she should do to get, or rather steal money for the house-keeping. And how did she do it, I hear you ask. She soon learnt to win the good graces of whoever came to my house, local or foreigner, by babbling on with one man or another, so that no one found anything better to do than flirt with her. I'd make her hold in her hand a china bowl broken into three pieces. And whenever a gentleman knocked at the door, she'd pull on a cord and run to the head of the stairs, all dishevelled, crying under her breath: 'Oh, I'm a dead woman! Oh, I've had it!' And while she was pretending she wanted to run away, my other, older maid would hold her firmly by the hem of her skirt, saying: 'Don't, don't do it, the mistress isn't going to hurt you.' The unthinking man, seeing her so upset, would grab her arm, all agitated, and say: 'What is it? Why all the crying? Why all the wailing?' and she'd reply: 'Poor me, I've broken this thing that's worth a ducat. Let go of me; she'll kill me if she catches me.' And she'd deliver these lies with such deft gesticulations, a few heartfelt sighs and simulated swooning, that it would have aroused compassion in Jack, the one-handed hangman, never mind my gentleman caller. All the while I stood at a peephole in my room, with my apron stuffed in my mouth so he wouldn't hear me laughing, whilst he, tighter than a clenched fist, slipped a scudo into her hand, putting it on the alms side of the ledger. And I thought I'd burst when my old maid snatched it from her and hurried down the stairs so he'd think she'd gone to buy another bowl.

PIPPA: What a crook!

NANNA: At that point I came into the room, and he said: 'I've come to pay my respects to Your Ladyship,' taking my hand and kissing it soggily. And when he'd stayed chatting to me for about twenty minutes, the girl would come in carrying the replacement for the broken bowl, saying: 'I'll just put it back in your room,' and I'd say: 'What's the matter with

you? Why do you look so sullen?' And the little rascal
would signal to him not to give the game away.

PIPPA: You'd need more skills than a doctor to be a courtesan.

NANNA: And so, adapting the ruse to every man who came
to see me, now holding a glass, now a cup, and now a plate
in her hand, she'd swindle sometimes two, four and even
five julios from this purse or that, and my housekeeping
would pay for some nice little banquets. Now for the
big one,

PIPPA: OK, I'll buy it, before you even start.

NANNA: An officer, a man whose position assured him an
income of around two thousand ducats, had fallen so madly
in love with me that his suffering could have atoned for all
his sins. This fellow spent money once in a blue moon, and
you had to be an astrologer, I can tell you, if you wanted to
get any out of him when he wasn't in the mood to give it
to you. In fact eccentricity itself didn't exist until the day
he was born, and at every little word spoken out of turn he
would fly into a rage. At the very least he would scare the
living daylights out of you by reaching for his dagger and
holding it to your face, and courtesans fled from him as
peasants do from the rain. But I had learnt to to be fearless
and stayed the course with him; and even though he played
his monkey tricks on me, I defended myself cunningly,
always thinking how I could put one over on him that
would pay him back for the lot. In the end, I thought so
hard I found the answer. And what did I do? I confided in
a painter – I may as well tell you: it was Master Andrea –
granting him a few little favours on the understanding that
he should do what I told him. So, hiding under my bed with
his paints and his brushes, he'd paint a gash on my face
when the time came. I also opened up to Dr Mercurio, of

blessed memory. You must have heard of him.

PIPPA: Of course.

NANNA: I told him I'd send for him one night and that he should come with some lint and eggs. So he didn't leave his house on the day of the sting. Now, picture the scene: Master Andrea is under my bed, and Dr Mercurio is waiting at home, and I'm at the table with the officer. When we'd almost finished eating, I happened to mention one of His Excellency's chamberlains, whom he hated hearing me talk about – doing it on purpose to tease him. Well, it doesn't take much of a spark to light dry straw, and while he was yelling: 'Slut, bitch, jezebel,' I tried to retort and he struck my cheek with the flat of his dagger, and I felt it, I can tell you. Now I had in my pocket some sort of oily varnish given to me by Master Andrea, and I smeared my hands and rubbed my face with it, and letting out the most terrifying shrieks ever to be heard from a woman in labour, made him believe that he'd caught me with the blade. Then, as scared as if he'd murdered someone, he took to his heels and fled to Cardinal Colonna's palace, where he locked himself in the room of his courtier friend, crying softly: 'Oh God, I think I've lost Nanna, Rome, and my commission.' Meanwhile, I shut myself in my bedroom with just my old maid; and Master Andrea, having been flushed from his hiding place, painted such a gash across my right cheek with a single stroke that, seeing myself in the mirror, I thought I'd faint from shock. At that point, Dr Mercurio, summoned by the little trickster of the broken bowl, came in, saying: 'Don't worry – no harm done.' Then, giving the paint time to dry, he took the lint and steeped it in rose oil and egg-white and, after bandaging the wound 'with grace and privilege'[11], moved into the living-room where a large crowd had gathered, and said: 'She won't live.' The news spread all over Rome; even the murderer heard an echo of it and wept like a smacked child. The next morning the doctor came and, holding a twopenny candle to it, removed the dressing, at which a great many people, craning their heads into the room, in which all the shutters had been closed, started to cry; and someone or other passed out, too squeamish to look at such a terrible wound. So it became public knowledge that my face – if the worst came to the worst – would be ruined for ever. And the villain, while sending me money, medicines and doctors, tried to take cover from the sheriff, not entirely reassured by Colonna's support. A week later, I gave the word that I had survived, though scarred, which is a fate worse than death for a courtesan; and our friend tried to soothe me with money, sparing no efforts and managing to enlist so many of his friends and patrons that I finally came to an agreement, though I never let anyone see me except a certain monsignor of ill repute who used to hang around with my friend. In short, five hundred ducats were disbursed for the damage and fifty more for doctors and medicines; and I forgave him – that is to say, I promised not to pursue charges against him with the governor, demanding only his assurance that I be left in peace. And that was the money that I spent on the house – apart from the garden, which I added on later.

PIPPA: You were a valiant man, Mummy, to perform a feat like that.

NANNA: We're not at the Alleluia yet, and if I were to tell you all my stories, we wouldn't be finished till next year. Believe you me, I haven't wasted my time – no, my dear, I haven't. Now let's move on.

PIPPA: I can see that straight away.

NANNA: So anyway, it seemed to me that this five hundred, plus the fifty, had only whetted my appetite, and I thought up a whorish trick of the utmost whorishness. And what do you think I did? I found a Neapolitan, the rascal to end all rascals, with a reputation for having the secret of banishing all traces of a scar left on one's face from a wound. He came to see me, saying: 'On payment of a deposit of a hundred scudi, I'll make sure there's no more trace of a scar than there is here,' displaying the open palm of his hand. I shrank away and said, with a feigned sigh: 'Go and tell this miracle to the man who is to blame for my being no longer...' and implying 'as I once was', I turned away and started sobbing quietly. The rogue, in his very respectable outfit, left me and went to visit the officer, who was in a tight spot, stating his claims as to what he could achieve. Now, as you can imagine, this tormented man, despairing of ever being able to enjoy me again, forked out the ton. But anyway, to cut a long story short, the scar that wasn't there was removed with holy water, sprinkled over my face six times, and a few words resembling the *mirabilia*, but actually meaning nothing at all. So the one hundred smackers (as the Greek said) ended up in my hands.

PIPPA: Most welcome they are, too, and a Happy Christmas to them all.

NANNA: But listen. When word spread that I was left without a blemish in the world, everyone who had some sort of scar on their mug trotted off to the rascal's room, as the Jews would trot off to the Messiah if he were to descend on the Jewish quarter; and the trickster, having loaded his purse with down payments, packed it in and left, because he reckoned that these other people had recompensed him in full for the ducats he had enabled me to earn.

PIPPA: Did the officer know it, hear it, and believe it?

NANNA: He knew it without knowing it, he heard it without hearing it and he believed it without believing it.

PIPPA: So that was that.

NANNA: There's a sting in the tail.

PIPPA: What, there's more?

NANNA: This is the best bit. After all these disbursements, for which they say he had to sell his knighthood, the big oaf was reconciled with me through some mediators and by means of letters and messages singing his passion; and while he was on his way to throw himself at my feet, in sackcloth and ashes, thinking up a few words on the way to get back in my good graces, he happened to pass the workshop of a painter who'd painted a picture of the miracle, which I had said I would carry to Loreto; and fixing his eyes on it, he saw himself, dagger in hand, scarring poor me. And this would have been nothing, if it weren't for the inscription:

I MADONNA NANNA,
ADORING MESSER MACO,
AND ALLOWING THE OLD MAN TO SIP
FROM MY HONEY-POT,
AS A REWARD FOR MY ADORATION,
RECEIVED FROM HIM THIS SCAR
THAT WAS HEALED BY THE VIRGIN
TO WHOM I DEDICATE THIS VOTIVE IMAGE.

PIPPA: Ha! Ha!

NANNA: When he'd read his own story, he had the same expression as excommunicated bishops do, when they read the epitaphs on the tombstones under the feet of the devils that thrash them;[12] and rushing back home at his wits' end, he promised me a new dress if I'd consent to remove his name from the picture.

PIPPA: Ha! Ha! Ha!

NANNA: The moral of the story is this: his thuggishness proved costly, and he ended up giving me the money to travel even to places I *hadn't* vowed to go; and not only did I not go to those places, but he was forced to pay so much money that I could have been absolved by the Pope himself.

PIPPA: Was he really so stupid that, even when he visited you, he didn't realise that your face had never been scarred?

NANNA: Listen to this, Pippa: I took something the same shape as the knife-blade, and bandaged it very tightly against my cheek, keeping it there all night, and as soon as he appeared, I removed the bandage. So for quite some time, when you saw the bruise around the swollen flesh, you'd have believed that it was indeed a healed cut.

PIPPA: Yes, that would work.

NANNA: I just want to tell you the one about the crane and then I'll finish today's lesson.

PIPPA: Go on, then, tell me.

NANNA: I pretended I had such cravings that you would be born with a birthmark[13] unless I was given a crane with pappardelle to eat; and not finding any at the market, one of my lovers was forced to send a man with a shotgun to kill one for me. But what did I do with it? I sent it to a pork-butcher who knew all my subjects (or 'vassals' as Gian Maria Giudeo called those from the Verucchio and the Scorticata hamlets). I forgot to mention: I made the man who gave me the crane swear not to say anything, and when he asked me why, I just told him I didn't want to be thought of as a glutton.

PIPPA: And rightly so. Now to the pork-butcher.

NANNA: I made him agree not to sell it to anyone apart from someone who would buy it for me, and having already been of service in such dealings in the past, he understood me at once. And as soon as he'd hung it in his shop, one of those who knew about my cravings approached him with: 'How much do you want for it?'; 'It's not for sale,' answered the crafty man to make him want it even more, so much so, in fact, that he'd have given anything to have it. And he kept pleading with him, saying: 'Money's no object.' He ended up paying out a ducat, and, sending it to my house with a valet, he tried to make me believe that a cardinal had given it to him. And when I'd made a fuss of him and he'd left, I sent it back to be resold. What do you think happened? The crane was bought by all my lovers, each time for a ducat, and brought back again and again to my house. So now, Pippa, would you say it's a doddle knowing how to make a living as a whore?

PIPPA: I'm amazed.

NANNA: Now, let's get on to the methods you should use to catch clients.

PIPPA: Yes, that's the most important bit.

NANNA: Suppose five or six new punters come to see you accompanied by one of your servants. Give them a lordly welcome, sit yourself down with them, and enter into pleasant conversation, as respectably as possible. And while you're chatting and listening, glance at their clothes and judge from their demeanour what you might be able to get out of them. And when you've politely dismissed the servant, probe each one as to his condition of life, then focus on your main aim. Start ogling the richest man, and flirt with him using amorous gestures, as if you were dying for his love; never lift your eyes from his without sighing. Make sure you only learn this man's name, and when they leave, say to him: 'I kiss Your Lordship So-and-So's hand,' and to the others: 'Nice to meet you.' Run to the blinds as soon as they leave the house and let yourself be seen only when he glances back to show his interest; and as you're about to lose sight of him, lean your whole body out of the window, wagging your finger in warning, to suggest that his divine presence has turned your heart upside down. You'll see he'll return to your house by himself, with more assurance than when he was accompanied; the rest is up to you, Pippa.

PIPPA: I love watching you talk.

NANNA: I want to tell you something else now before I forget. Never laugh while whispering to someone sat next to you, whether at table, or by the fire, or anywhere else, because it's one of the worst flaws in a woman, either gentlewoman or whore – you can't prevent all and sundry suspecting that they're being made fun of, and it's often the cause of the most violent rifts. Also, don't order your servants around, like a queen, while others are present; instead, do whatever you can yourself. People know quite well that you have servants and that you can order them around, so if you don't boss them about in a haughty way, you'll be thought well of, and whoever sees you will say: 'Oh, what a kind person – how gracefully she deigns to do everything.' But if they hear you losing your temper, and threatening them for not running to pick up a toothpick that dropped from your hand or not buffing one of your slippers, they'll think woe betide anyone who has you as a mistress, and they'll wink at each other over your arrogance.

PIPPA: Wise words, good words.

NANNA: But I mustn't forget to tell you how to behave at a

banquet where there'll be a whole pack of courtesans, who are by nature always envious, cold, touchy and fussy. You'll understand when I'm no longer here.

PIPPA: Why do you say that?

NANNA: I'm saying it so I won't have to say it in future. Anyway, here you are at a feast – it's Carnival-time and all sorts of ladies have been invited; they appear masked up in the ballroom, dancing, sitting around and talking, all without taking their masks off. And they're right not to while all the people who aren't invited to dinner enjoy the music and dancing; but later on, when people have washed their hands, they're wrong not to eat at the table with everyone else, one woman going this way and another going that. You'd need to be a magician to conjure up all the rooms needed to satisfy those who want to dine alone with their lovers, upsetting the dinner, the party, the household, the servants, the butlers, and the cooks – may God poison all the rest of their birthdays, and many happy returns to them.

PIPPA: Fussy cows!

NANNA: Not to worry, I'll teach you how to steal every man's heart with your gentle ways.

PIPPA: Really?

NANNA: Definitely.

PIPPA: Tell me, then, please.

NANNA: Go straight to table, without waiting to be asked twice, and sit where they tell you, as if to say: 'Here I am, just as my mother made me.' If you do this, you'll be praised to high heaven, from here to the spits in the kitchen.

PIPPA: Why do the women run off to other rooms?

NANNA: Because they're afraid of comparisons. No one wants to be called wrinkly; no ugly woman can bear having a beautiful one sat next to her; no woman with rotten teeth wants to open her mouth next to one whose teeth are as white as snow; and if a woman can't afford the gown, necklace, sash or coif worn by some other woman – though she thinks herself a nonpareil and the best of the bunch in all other respects – she'd rather die than let herself be seen in public. Some hide because they're worthless, some because they're mad, and others because they're malicious. And another thing: when they're off by themselves, they say the worst things they can possibly think up about each other: 'That string of pearls isn't hers; that gown belongs to another man's wife; that ruby came from Messer Picciuolo, and that thing from the Jew.' And so they get more drunk on gossip than they do on wine. But they get it back in spades from the men dining with you – one man says: 'Lady So-and-So does well to hide her bad manners,' another one cries: 'Oh, Lady Such-and-Such, when did you take your decoction of lignum vitae[14]?' Others laugh fit to burst because they've recognised 'Aunt Flo' in this or that woman's eyes. Others regard the good Mr What's-his-name as a man of enormous courage for daring to sleep beside his goddess who looks not even like a she-devil, but like the very devil himself. In the end, turning to you, they'll offer their body and soul.

PIPPA: Thanks very much.

NANNA: When you find yourself in this situation, do yourself honour, and you'll honour me. Now, you'll go to Santa Maria del Popolo, the Consolazione, St Peter's, St John's and other principal churches on solemn feast-days, and there you'll find a host of all the gallant lords, courtiers, and noblemen crowding into the places they can most easily spot the beauties from, trying a line on all the women who pass by or who dip their fingers into the font – and getting the occasional stinging pinch. As you pass by, be graceful; don't answer back with the arrogance of a whore, but either keep quiet or say, with real or feigned reverence, 'Your servant.' By saying this you'll avenge yourself with your modesty, and when you return they'll all make way for you and bow down to the ground. If you answer them curtly, they'll blow raspberries at you for the whole length of the church, and that will be that.

PIPPA: I can well believe it.

NANNA: And as you kneel down on the predella of the most conspicuous altar in the church, strike a pious pose, with your prayer book in hand.

PIPPA: What would I be doing with a book when I don't know how to read?

NANNA: Making it look as if you can, and it doesn't even matter if you're holding it upside down, like those Roman women do to make people believe they're clairvoyant, though they're actually just spooks. Now, let's get onto the qualities of the youngsters – never pin your hopes on them, or rely on their promises; they're not dependable, but, changeable as their fickle minds and their hot blood, they fall in and out of love with the first woman they meet. Even if you only give them a bit every now and then, make them pay upfront. And you'll be sorry if you get entangled, either with them or anyone else; falling in love is all well and good for those who are independently wealthy, but not for those who have to scrape by from day to day. And the worst of it is, as soon as you've let yourself get ensnared, you're done for, because if you set your heart on just one man, all those other chaps you used to caress even-handedly will be getting ideas. In fact, you could say that a courtesan whose heart pounds for anything other than her purse is like a greedy, drunken tavern-keeper, who, instead of denying himself, eats and drinks what he should be selling.

PIPPA: You really, really do know everything.

NANNA: I think I hear a captain breaking down your door (God, nowadays everyone calls himself 'Captain' – I reckon that even mule-drivers achieve captaincy). I say 'breaking down', because they beat with bravado, just to seem tough, talking all the while in a gibberish made up of some Spanish phrases and a few French ones mixed in. Don't waste your time with these blowhards. Even if you love them, trust them as much as you would trust a gypsy; they're worse than coal – you'll either get burnt or smudged. They croak away about waiting for their stipends; and if you're happy to wait for the invasions they want the King to undertake and the victories Mother Church will score before you get paid, then go ahead and waste your time cosseting them; but if it's money you're after, then praise them like the great champion Orlando and run away quickly, otherwise you'll leave with a broken head, as you would hanging around those reckless young rascals – the greatest honour they'll pay you is to proclaim the defects of your front entrance and back entrance, boasting about how nicely they make you heave and shake.

PIPPA: Stupid clowns!

NANNA: A woman who becomes a whore to satisfy her lust and not her hunger is getting herself into deep water; if she wants to throw off her rags – if she wants, I repeat, to get rid of her tatters – she should wise up and not muck about, in word or deed. Here's a nice little comparison for you, hot off the press – I improvise as I talk, you see, rather than winching out what I can say in a single breath, or taking a hundred years like some speechifying student of a pedagogic hack, hiring out the 'I shall speak', the 'I shall go' and the 'I shall shit', and composing comedies out of phrases more constipated than constipation. That's why everyone rushes to read my gossip, putting it in print as if it were the *Verbum Caro*[15].

PIPPA: Now – the little comparison.

NANNA: You know, a soldier who is capable only of stealing chickens from peasants' coops and scaring prison chaplains is considered a good-for-nothing and will never be hired, so a man from the Guard told me. He also said that a soldier who goes into battle and proves his ability is sought after by all the armies and paymasters in the world. So, too, a whore who only knows how to be worked over and nothing more, will never get rid of her threadbare fans and calico gowns. So, my dear, you need either art or luck; and if I had to ask straight out, I'd say I'd rather have luck than art.

PIPPA: Why?

NANNA: Because there's no effort with luck, but art makes you sweat, and you need to be able to read the stars and live by your wits, as I think I've already said. And as proof that with luck there are no obstacles, just look at that good-for-nothing lousy bitch – you know the one – and you'll see.

PIPPA: Oh, isn't she filthy rich?

NANNA: That's what I mean: she has no grace, no talent, not a single redeeming feature; no figure, she's awkward, over thirty, and yet, despite all this, she must have honey down there, the way they all run after her. Luck, eh? Luck? Ask her servants, the lads, the procurers – don't make me tell you – her luck makes them gentlemen and monsignors, we see it every day. Luck? Luck, eh? Messer Troiano used to carve grinding-bowls; now he owns a fine palace. Luck, eh? Luck? Serapica groomed dogs and then was made Pope. Luck? Luck, eh? Acursio was an errand boy for a goldsmith and then became Julius II.[16] Luck, eh? Luck? And, to be sure, when you find both luck and art together in a whore, then *sursum corda!*[17] Because that's even more satisfying than the 'Right there, right there!' you cry the moment the finger, that's been scratching around, following the 'lower, higher, this way a bit, that way a bit', finds the pimple that's torturing you. Lucky her who has both. Art and luck, eh? Luck and art, eh?

PIPPA: Go back, though, to where you left off.

NANNA: I left off as I was discouraging you from friendships with gluttonous young louts and so-called captains. And I was telling you to keep away from them, as I'm now going to tell you to go after sober men, because they'll give you as much money as good manners.

PIPPA: A few more pennies and a little less politeness would go down well.

NANNA: Of course, but sober men will give you both, and continually; and so the sweet-natured fellow is our business, for if she earns a living from men like these, a woman will have the same satisfaction as a wet-nurse who suckles, looks after and brings up a lice-free kiddy who never cries, day or night. But now to the fussy ones – spare us! With these types, strip away your pride – which we whores carry from the cunt that shat us out – and whenever these bores speak to you in a surly way, yell at you, scold you or offend you with their jokes, be on your guard as if you were a bear-baiter. Take care that the jackasses don't land their kicks and make sure some of their pelt is always left behind in your hands.

PIPPA: Damn me if I don't.

NANNA: After these beasts come the swordsmen – those home-and-tavern heroes who wouldn't have the courage to stick it up Castruccio's arse.[18] They never stop their big talk – they'll offer you the moon on a stick. Oh, won't you be greater than Ancroia[19] if you can get them out of their coats of mail and the swords they wear so pointlessly at their sides?

PIPPA: So I shall.

NANNA: Between one species and the other come the jokers, just out to have a good laugh; and with that 'Ha! Ha! Ha!' which spills out so thoughtlessly, they'll describe in block capitals what they did with you and what they want to do, and they'll talk louder the more people are there, regardless of who they are; they do it by nature and to show their good humour, and they'd lift your skirts in company as soon as spit on the ground. You should insult them, ruffling them with the same boldness they ruffle you; and you can get away with it, because they don't take notice of anything – they exist without a care in the world.

PIPPA: Do you think such company will suit me?

NANNA: You're like me in your tastes. But tell me, haven't I told you that eccentric men are like monkeys that can be pacified with a nut? Even the sea, which is such a wild beast, makes less noise than a brook once its anger subsides.

PIPPA: Yes, I think you did.

NANNA: Of course I did, but I didn't mention the ignoramuses. As for them – worse than the villains, the asses, the wretches, the brutes, the hypocrites, the pedants, the misers and the rest of the human race – I don't know how to advise you. They turn up their noses even at the best, and every favour you do them is a wasted effort; the swines will pounce on you without a moment's thought, and every move they make, much to your harm and shame, is proof of their stupidity.

PIPPA: Why my harm and shame?

NANNA: Because they have neither manners nor wit, and will always try to sit above the salt, speak when they should be silent and keep quiet when they should speak; thus depriving you of the company of decent people. And anyone who's seen them flirting among the ladies can see they're like pigs sniffing roses in a garden; make sure you break their bones with the cudgel of prudence.

PIPPA: I'll break their hearts as well. But aren't the eccentrics just the same as the crackpots?

NANNA: Exactly – the crackpots are worse than clocks that don't keep time, and you should avoid them more than raving madmen. They want it, then they don't want it; one moment they're silent and the next they're deafening you with their chatter; most of the time they're in a mood without knowing why. And St Nafissa, who was patience and kindness itself, wouldn't have been able to live with their quirks; so, from the first moment you meet them, be like oil on water – don't mix with them.

PIPPA: I'll do as you say.

NANNA: And what about those born-and-bred know-it-alls? What cruelty, what penance it is to have to preside over those smart alecs; they never speak, for fear of unfurling the lips they've spent time in front of the mirror arranging; and if they do speak, they open their mouths with such care that their lips fall back exactly into place; and they're always taking your words the wrong way, eating professorially, spitting perfect spheres and looking down their noses. They want to be seen with whores but would prefer it not to get out. They're careful not to give you money in the presence of the servants, but make sure the servants realise they're giving it to you.

PIPPA: So what kind of men are they?

NANNA: If anyone turns up while they're in your house, they'll hide in your room, and they'll peek through the cracks in the door, working themselves into a state until you tell the man they're hiding from: 'Messer is in the room.' On top of that, they keep a tally of their sleeping, waking, eating, fasting, going, staying, doing it, not doing it, talking, keeping quiet, laughing, not laughing, and everything is done so simperingly, that they would surpass even a new bride. But this is nothing. It all becomes too much when they needle you and you're forced to account for the money you've made and your intentions as to your savings. And, since this wise man – or rather this man who thinks himself wise – is also a bit of a miser, play him at his own game and embroider the effort it takes to earn the money. And, fabricating every act, be like the Capranica think tank[20], outdoing Solomon himself. I have it from a good source that there are no follies more witless than those of the wise, even when they're not in love – so think what follies they get up to when they're head over heels.

PIPPA: And think what I'll do to them, once those chumps are caught in my web!

NANNA: Have I told you anything about hypocrites?

PIPPA: No, ma'am.

NANNA: Hypocrites, who'll only touch themselves down there if they're wearing gloves, and are devoutly devotional every Friday in March and on Ember Days, will come to see you on the sly; and if, after they've requested the honour of taking the back road, you say: 'What, like that, from behind?' they'll reply: 'We're only human.' Pippa, little one, keep these people's business secret, and don't spill the beans about their dirty ways – it's for your own good. These scoundrels, these enemies of faith, suck, grope and penetrate every hole and crack just like any other good-for-nothing, and when they find a woman who knows how to hush up the sleazy habits they delight in, they'll give it their all without holding back. Then, as they retie their codpieces, they'll babble on, reciting the *miserere*, the *domine ne in furore* and the *exaudi orationem*,[21] and then set off to scratch the itches of lepers.

PIPPA: May they be flayed alive!

NANNA: They'll suffer worse one day, no doubt; and their mean little souls will be trampled underfoot by those other greedy, miserable pigs who'd be scrounging money even while they're fucking. To make scoundrels like that put out, you need the same cunning they use in stowing it away. Oh, what punishment it is to have to snatch money from their fists! And don't be thinking they'll let the pears fall from the tree, even after a good shake. Even the most loving of mothers won't mollycoddle her little son who won't fall asleep or eat his pap as you must do a miser. As he pulls out a coin, his fingers will start trembling, and he'll gaze longingly at every worn-out penny he gives you. With these scoundrels set your snares and catch the coots in a trap like you'd catch an old fox; and if you want them to come up with the goods, don't ask for too much, but drink their blood sip by sip, saying: 'I can't have it made, because I'm five measly ducats short.'

PIPPA: What, a dress?

NANNA: Yes, a dress. And as you say this, you'll see him writhe like a man who wants to relieve himself and can't find anywhere to do it; and as he's squirming and mumbling he'll scratch his head, pull at his beard and frown like a stepmother, as a gambler does when he's got a hand that's neither good nor bad, but has to play on anyway. So then he'll pay up, grumbling, and as soon as you have the money, shower him with kisses and a thousand caresses. Keep that up for about three days, then begin to sigh, chew your nails, and stop looking pleased to see him; and if he asks: 'What's wrong?' answer him with: 'My rotten luck, which is the reason I'm barefoot and naked, and it's all because I'm too thrifty. If I weren't, less than four scudi wouldn't even keep me in *this* ugly skirt.' Having no alternative, the miserable good-for-nothing will say: 'You never get your fill, and then you throw money down the toilet. Here, take it, and get off my back – I'm not giving you another penny.' And tying up his purse again, he'll hurry off to find some way of pilfering it back from someone else.

PIPPA: Why not ask for all of it at once?

NANNA: Because you'll frighten him with the amount.

PIPPA: I see.

NANNA: Now, with generous men what is needed is the cunning of a fox, not an ass. And, whenever you ask for anything, ask them *coram populo*[22], because these windbags grow an inch taller when you treat them like lords in public – giving is in the nature of lords, though they don't always demonstrate it; so without even asking, you just need to say: 'I want to buy a beautiful dress,' and they'll reply: 'If it's for a party, go ahead – I want you to have it.' With men like this, my dear, you should also be generous – whatever position they put you in, stay put, and don't ever deny them what their appetites demand.

PIPPA: That's only fair.

NANNA: Beware of those who wouldn't give you a grain of

rice even if you asked for it; others wouldn't give you a pittance if you weren't there digging them in the ribs. Don't order courteous men about, just let them do what comes naturally, which is revelling in constantly giving you things. They think that giving you things without being asked is money spent not on whoring, but on earning their lordly reputations, since, as I have said, giving should be in the nature of lords. So, with men like this, all you have to do is please and respect them, and not just say: 'Give me this; do that for me'; though when they do give you this and do that, you should pretend you don't want them to.

PIPPA: Very well.

NANNA: As for the numbskulls (as they say in Rome), never stop hounding them with 'give me this, do that for me', because these jackasses need prodding. And if there are others around when you say it, they're thrilled, because it makes them look experienced and not like simpletons. Besides, they think it gives them the air of a great scholar, having the lady herself implore them, and though they're like ants in a tree trunk about to burst, if you keep knocking, they'll come out.

PIPPA: They'll have to come out or they'll die.

NANNA: While I remember – although I use both the familiar and formal addresses when I speak, make sure you use only the formal with every man, young or old, noble or commoner, because the familiar sounds curt and people don't like it very much. And of course good manners are the best sponsors for rising up in the world, so never be presumptuous in your ways and keep to the proverb that says: 'Never mock at the truth and never do harm with a joke.' When you're with your lover's friends or associates, never let a prickly word slip from your mouth or ever get the urge to pull someone's hair or beard, or give them a little slap, soft or hard, because men are men, and if you touch their faces, they'll twist their snouts and snort as if they were mortally offended. I've seen some brutish gestures, and even blows, let fly at some annoying woman who felt so sure of herself that she tweaked the men's ears; and they all said: 'You asked for that.'

PIPPA: She certainly did.

NANNA: Another thing I ought to remind you of: don't follow the same path as a common whore, whose idea of loyalty is never being loyal – rather die than jilt anyone; only make promises you can keep, and whichever punter comes your way, don't kiss goodbye to any other man who deserves to sleep with you, unless the Frenchman I mentioned before comes for you. If he turns up, send for the man who was supposed to be with you that evening and say: 'I've promised you this night and it's yours, because I'm completely yours; but I could earn a nice little profit with it and if you'll allow me this one night, I'll repay you with a hundred. A monsignor from France wants me tonight and, if you agree, I'll give it to him, but if you don't, here I am at Your Lordship's command.' Seeing himself highly regarded, he'll sagely grant you what's not his to grant, and bow to your wishes, and, in addition to this favour, he'll become your slave. But if you were to dump him without a word, you'd run the risk of losing him; and what's more, as he went around complaining about your rudeness, all those who had taken a fancy to you would take a disliking.

PIPPA: So you mean it would be like adding insult to injury?

NANNA: You've said it. Now listen carefully: occasionally you will be surrounded by all your lovers, and you should be aware that if your favours are not equally distributed, the fellow who gets least will have his nose put out of joint. So weigh your favours out on the scales of discretion; and if it happens that you feel more inclined to one than another, fake it; show your inclination with small signals and not wild gestures, making sure some other man does not go away angry with you or your favourite. Every punter deserves a go, and while the one who gives most should also receive most, you should be gracious about it. For every country in the world there is a road – so act wisely, live wisely, be wise.

PIPPA: I shall do it par excellence.

NANNA: Now this is an important point: don't take pleasure in upsetting friendships by reporting gossip; avoid scandals; and whenever you can make peace, do so. And even if your door is smeared with tar or set alight, laugh it off – this is just the fruit of those trees that lovers plant in whores' gardens. No matter how vicious their actions or their words, never come to blows with those you can command. If someone upsets you, keep quiet – don't run crying to tell the man who's dying with love for you and fuming with rage. And when one of those lechers comes to your house, don't ever say a bad word about the woman he's fallen out with, when it's easily made up, to the shame and detriment of those who stoked the fire; instead, scold him and say: 'You are wrong to be angry with her, for she is beautiful, virtuous, respectable and as graceful as a woman can be.' The outcome will be that this man, returning to the trough the next day, will feel obliged to you, and the woman, who'll have heard all about it, will pay you back in kind if one of your lovers happens to be in a mood with you.

PIPPA: I know how sharp you are.

NANNA: Now, my dear, here's something to think about: if

I, the most wicked and villainous whore in all of Rome, in fact in all of Italy, or the world even, managed to get myself covered with gold rather than copper, whilst doing evil, speaking worse, betraying friends and foes and well-wishers without a second thought, imagine what you can achieve, if you follow my teaching.

PIPPA: I'll be the queen of queens, not just the lady of ladies.

NANNA: So take my advice.

PIPPA: I will.

NANNA: Yes do – and don't waste your time gambling, because cards and dice make paupers out of those who get mixed up with them, and for every courtesan who scores a new cape, there are a thousand who leave as beggars. It's okay to have a chess- and draughtboard for display; and when only a julio or two are at stake that's enough to cover the candles, because the little they win they'll give to Your Ladyship; and if you avoid playing *condennata* or *primiera*[23], you'll never hear an argument, and no one will start swearing. And if a man who is keen on a flutter is in love with you, ask him gently, but for all to hear, to give up playing – pretend you're doing this to stop him ruining himself, not so that he'll give you the money.

PIPPA: Got it.

NANNA: Scold your man as well if he gives you too much to eat – pretend not to like it and disguise your greed. And the best advice I can give you is to take pleasure in having worthy people in your house – even if they are not in love with you, they'll attract lovers to you by their presence and win you honour among others. Dress simply and neatly; embroidery is a waste of money and workmanship – it costs an arm and a leg and, when you try to resell it, you won't get anything for it. And velvet and satin spoilt by the threads of trimmings you've removed, are worse than tatters. So be frugal, because at the end of the day our dresses can be converted into money.

PIPPA: Suits me.

NANNA: Now we come on to accomplishments, of which whores are as much the natural enemies as they are of someone who approaches them empty-handed. Pippa, no man will refuse you a little instrument, so ask one for a lute, another for a harpsichord, this man a viola, that man a flute, this one a little organ and that one a lyre – these are all just a perk of the job. Invite the masters to come and teach you the notes, keep them amused and make them play certain passages for you, paying them with hopes and promises and a few meals on the hoof. After you've done the instruments, move on to paintings and sculpture, extorting pictures, plates, portraits, busts, nudes and whatever you can, because they'll sell for at least as much as the dresses.

PIPPA: Isn't it shameful to sell the clothes off your back?

NANNA: Why shameful? Isn't it more of a disgrace to gamble them away, the way they did those of Our Lord?

PIPPA: You're right.

NANNA: Cards are the devil's books – so I tell you again, don't keep cards or dice in the house; one glimpse of them, and anyone given to gambling is as good as done for. I swear to you by the eve of St Lena of the Oil that they poison the minds of bystanders the same way plague-ridden clothes infect people who touch them even after they've been locked away for ten years.

PIPPA: Cards and dice, begone!

NANNA: Now listen – listen to what I have to tell you about the pomp and circumstance of festivals. Pippa, don't get caught up in bull-roping or quintains or ring-tilting, because they cause deadly feuds and are no more than an amusement for brats and riff-raff. If you really want to see a bit of killing and a bit of running about after this and that, go and watch the games at other people's houses. And when you borrow capes or thoroughbred horses for masquerades, look after them as if they were your own, and when you give them back, don't send them off without cleaning them, as common whores usually do, but make sure they are well groomed and refolded as they were before; otherwise their owners will bear a terrible grudge; and often get angry with whoever suggested that they lend them to you.

PIPPA: Don't imagine I'm that shoddy – only an ass wouldn't do that.

NANNA: An absolute ass. Now, if I were to tell you all about how to wear your hair and how to leave a little lock hanging down over your forehead or curling round your eye so that it opens and closes with a cheeky wink, I'd be prattling on till nightfall. Likewise if I wanted to teach you how to arrange your tits so that a man, seeing them on the flap of your blouse, will stare hard, trying to peer inside as far as possible; be thrifty with them just as some are overgenerous – like those women who look as if they're trying to throw them away and have them jumping out of their stays and bodices. As it is, I'll be finished in one or two more breaths – three at the most.

PIPPA: I wouldn't mind if you kept on for a whole year.

NANNA: Anything I've forgotten to tell you, and anything I don't know, whoredom itself will teach you; it has its own resources, which spring forth all at once, unexpected by others and unthought of by you, so you'll have to compensate for my bad memory with your good instincts. But I haven't told you…

PIPPA: What?

NANNA: The priests and monks were trying to pick a hole in my brain and slip through the gap.

PIPPA: Oh, those rogues.

NANNA: Filthy, dirty rogues, you mean.

PIPPA: Since you've already taught me how I should go on with men like that, I want to know how much it'll hurt when they take my virginity.

NANNA: Not at all, only a bit.

PIPPA: Will it make me shriek like someone having a boil pierced?

NANNA: Certainly not!

PIPPA: Like someone having a dislocated hand fixed?

NANNA: Less than that.

PIPPA: Like a tooth being pulled?

NANNA: Less.

PIPPA: Like cutting a finger?

NANNA: No.

PIPPA: Like when you crack your head?

NANNA: You're not even close.

PIPPA: Like an ingrowing toenail?

NANNA: Do you want me to bring it home to you properly?

PIPPA: Yes.

NANNA: Do you ever remember scratching a rash like mild scabies?

PIPPA: I do remember.

NANNA: That burning feeling you get after scratching is like the pain you feel when your hymen is torn.

PIPPA: Then why are girls so frightened of losing their virginity? I've heard that some girls jump out of bed, some scream for help, and others bleed all over the chests, the room and whatever's closest.

NANNA: It's just the fear of those who don't know what to expect. It was quite common in the old days, when brides went to their weddings wearing pointy hats and a cock was flung out of the window to announce the wedding. There's no difference between the regret one feels at not having had a tooth pulled earlier, while someone else holds in their hand the tooth that has caused them so much pain, and the regret of girls who have put off having their quim rubbed for fear that: 'It'll hurt'. A girl who has bravely had it in her will say: 'And I thought doing the deed was a big deal.'

PIPPA: I'm glad to hear it.

NANNA: The day before you come on the market, I'll teach you how you can fake virginity as many times as you need – the secret lies in rock alum and pine resin boiled together; it's a little trick used in all the best brothels.

PIPPA: Sounds good to me.

NANNA: Now to the monks – even from here I'm choking on their stench of goats, gruel, gravy and pork; though there are still a few well-dressed ones, and some who are sweeter-smelling than a perfumery.

PIPPA: Don't get off the point – I want you to tell me how to put on and take off make-up; I also want to know if I should believe in spells, witchcraft and other charms, or not.

NANNA: Don't talk such foolish nonsense: my fresh and tasty advice will be all the charm you need; as for grooming yourself I'll tell you how to do it. But the monks are calling, and urging me to tell you how come women smell a bit off to them these days – it all comes down to the priests, the primates, the priors, the ministers, the curates, and the rest of the rabble belonging to the league of reverends and right reverends. When they sleep with a woman they have about as much appetite as someone who's been gorging his guts. And even if you sing them that song that's meant for old men:

Snail, snail,
Put out your horns,
I'll give you bread
And barleycorns.

it doesn't prick up until they sleep with their little husbands.

PIPPA: Oh, do monks and priests have husbands, then?

NANNA: If only they chose to have wives!

PIPPA: Hellfire!

NANNA: Shall I tell you or not?

PIPPA: Why wouldn't you?

NANNA: Because the truth got Christ crucified. But anyway I've told you now, and it's a fine state of affairs that lies bring advantages and the truth gets you a slap in the face. Whoever calls me an old whore and a thieving bawd is a bad mouth. That's why I'm telling you that the big fish in the monasteries and the priesthood hire courtesans just to watch them being screwed by their rent boys, yes, rent boys; and it whets their appetites to see them penetrated *per alia via* (as the Epistle says). But keep these boys as friends, and go whenever they call you, because old What's-his-name, who'll let them do whatever they want with you, is easily led, and will throw all the earnings of the bishopric, the abbey, the chapter house and the order at you.

PIPPA: If I hang around with them, I'll get it all, including the belfry.

NANNA: You'll be doing no more than your duty, if you do. Ha! Ha! Ha! I'm laughing at the merchants – we haven't got on to them yet, have we?

PIPPA: Yes we have.

NANNA: You mean the Germans. Almost all of *them* work for other people, so they are careful not to visit you, as I've said. I'm talking about the great merchants, the moneymakers – may they all be struck down with hernias for the pittance they dole out and expect whores to manage on. For every man who spends, there are always twenty ready with: 'I've put it all in usury, I mean high-yield investments', whenever you ask them for something. But the worst of it is that they go bankrupt on a full purse, walling themselves up in their houses or burying themselves alive in churches; then they say: 'That bloody whore has ruined me.' I'm telling you, Pippa, you should give them the boot, though some fat-headed women, God knows why, believe that being friends with them swells their reputation, and when anyone asks: 'Who's he?' they imagine that the fact that he's a merchant apotheosises them as goddesses – but it's worth nothing, nothing at all, I swear.

PIPPA: I believe you.

NANNA: It takes more than gloves, letters of exchange and a ring on the finger to impress us.

PIPPA: I agree.

NANNA: My dear, I've told you a story fit for a queen, and don't imagine that mothers like yours grow on trees. I know of no preacher in Maremma who could have given you the sermon I have, and if you keep it well in mind, then slap me in the pillory if you're not adored as the richest and cleverest courtesan that ever was, is, or shall be. So when I die, I'll die happy. And bear in mind that the stench, the snot, the gob, the revolting breath, filth, the habits and language of your lovers are like rancid wine: after drinking it for three days you forget the smell. But now listen to another couple of words about another couple of things.

Pippa: About what?

Nanna: The first is that you should not keep velvet pillows on silken beds – conceited sluts throw them on the floor and make their suitors kneel on them (filthy bitches, you'll end up starving on the carts). The next thing is that you should look after your hands; dip them carefully into your perfume jars; and don't daub your face like those clowns from Lombardy: a little touch of rouge is enough to dispel the pallor that often covers your cheeks after a bad night's sleep, an illness, or too much how's-your-father. In the morning, before breakfast, rinse out your mouth with water from the well; and if you want your skin to be clear and glowing and to stay that way, I'll give you my book of recipes, which will teach you how to take care of your complexion and keep your skin lovely. And I'll show you how to make a wonderful beauty lotion; and for your hands I'll give you a very, very delicate wash. I've also got something you can put in your mouth, which not only keeps your teeth white, but also gives your breath the fragrance of carnations. I'm amazed at some of those battered cods who paint and varnish themselves like the masquers in Modena, coating their lips in cinnabar so that whoever kisses them feels a strange burning on their own lips; and the breath, the teeth and the wrinkles on those women, caused by too much make-up! Pippa…

Pippa: Yes, ma'am?

Nanna: …don't use musk, civet, or other pungent perfumes,

because they're used to cover up the stench of people who stink. Hot towels, by all means; and wash and rewash as often as you can – washing in water boiled with aromatic herbs leaves the same sweetness in the flesh as you get from freshly washed linen when it's taken out of the chest and unfolded. And just as someone seeing its whiteness will feel drawn to rub his face in it, so, too, a man who catches sight of a lily-white breast, neck, and cheeks won't be able to stop himself kissing them again and again. And to make sure your teeth are well cleaned, before you get up, take the hem of the sheet and rub them with it several times to remove all the bits that are stuck, while they're still soft, before the air gets to them. But a load of good tips have suddenly dawned on me just as I wanted to finish up and say: 'I can't think of anything else to tell you.' But of course I am a deep, dark well, with a vein so large that the more water you draw, the more there is. Now, tie this knot in your handkerchief.

PIPPA: It's tied.

NANNA: As St Philip's day approaches, tell your lovers that you have taken a vow to pay for twenty masses on the eve of your saint's day, and also to feed ten paupers; and plant them with the cost. Then, on the eve and the feast-day itself, grumble and make a fuss, saying: 'I'll have to keep that burden on my soul now.' 'But why?' the suckers will ask. 'Because the priests are out collecting alms today and tomorrow and can't serve my masses.' Then, postponing it for another time, you'll be left with the money and your reputation intact.

PIPPA: That suits me.

NANNA: If you happen to have a crowd of lovers and gentlemen in your house who've come to keep your company, pretend you feel like going for a stroll for a couple of hours.

Spruce yourself up nonchalantly – don't waste time with frills and furbelows – then out the door you go with them, saying: 'Let's go to Santa Maria della Pace.' After you've recited a few lines of the Our Father there, take the Pilgrim's road and, stopping at every draper's shop, get them to trot out whatever luxuries and concoctions, amber scents and other fripperies they stock. And when you see something you want, don't say: 'Buy me this' or 'Buy me that', but: 'I like this and that', and have them set aside for you, saying: 'I'll send for them', and do the same with the perfumes and similar trifles.

PIPPA: What are you aiming at?

NANNA: I'm aiming straight at their dicky-bird.

PIPPA: With what crossbow?

NANNA: The crossbow of their own generosity, which would think itself slighted if they didn't buy the things reserved for you then and there, or soon after, at least, and give them to you as gifts.

PIPPA: If they're not wise to it, so much the worse for them.

NANNA: When you get home, distil your favours drop by drop exactly as I tell you.

PIPPA: You've already told me about favours.

NANNA: I've told you once, now I want to tell you all over again – knowing how to charm people is like an antidote to the evil eye. So sit yourself on a very low stool and sit two of your lovers at your feet, while you sit between two others, stretching out your arms to give them each a hand. Turn to one man, then another, and satisfy two more with your conversation. Favour all the rest with your glances and flirty winks, and make them think your heart is in your eyes and not in your hands, feet, or words. In this way you'll score eight simpletons in one stroke with the skill of your charms.

PIPPA: Two at a time.

NANNA: And even if you don't fancy one or other of them, force yourself. Model yourself on the sick man who takes his medicine reluctantly to cure his illness – you, too, will be cured, and not just of poverty (since if you become more than just a common whore you'll be rich), but also of the taint of being a courtesan, since you'll be a lady in deed, if not in name.

PIPPA: If believing in it counts, then I'm one already.

NANNA: Now, keep this one in mind: don't allow yourself to be led on by men who'll do anything to keep you for themselves. Don't trust them, no matter how rich or noble they may be – they get carried away by the fever of love and the frenzy of jealousy, and for as long as it lasts they'll move heaven and earth. Angela Greca can swear to this – she was left pushing up the daisies. What matters most is to find a constant supply of men, because the infatuated ones come and go. And even if there were nothing else to be gained from giving yourself to lots of men, at least you'll become more beautiful – just as you see with uninhabited houses that are aged by cobwebs; and swords, that get an extra shine after a good polishing.

PIPPA: That's true.

NANNA: Many accomplish much and few accomplish little – anyone who doubts that is an ass. What I want is for you to be a she-wolf that goes after a whole flock of sheep, not just one on its own. I have to warn you, my dear, though Envy herself was a whore, and is therefore the favourite pet of whores, keep her locked away inside you; and when you hear or see Lady Tullia and Lady Beatricicca flaunting their tapestries, capes, jewels and gowns, show how happy you are for them, and say: 'Of course, virtues and graces like theirs deserve even greater rewards. God bless the generosity of whoever gave them these gifts.' In return, both parties will favour you with a great affection – as great as the hate they would show you if you were to turn up your nose and say: 'Look there goes Queen Isolde herself – there'll come a day when she won't even be able to afford a candle to go for a shit with.' And believe you me, the torture one whore suffers at seeing another well dressed is worse than an old ache left over from the French disease lurking in the ankle of a foot or the ligament of a knee or the joint of an arm – not to put too fine a point on it, worse than one of those splitting headaches St Cosma and St Damiano used to cure.[24]

PIPPA: Let's wish those pains on the priests.

NANNA: Now, let's get on to the devotions necessary to body and soul. I want you to fast not on Saturdays – like those whores trying to outdo the Old Testament – but on the eves of feast-days, on all four Ember Days and every Friday in March; and start a rumour that you're not sleeping with anyone on those holy nights. Meanwhile, sell them off secretly to whoever will pay the most, but be careful that your other lovers don't catch you red-handed.

PIPPA: Even if I'm caught and fined, it'll have been worth it.

NANNA: Take note of this little ploy. Once in a while pretend to be ill and stay in bed for a couple of days, half dressed, so that, while you lie around receiving homage like a lady, the fine wines, young capons and other delicacies will start rolling in – for tricks like this you don't need to say a single word: it just takes a little posturing.

PIPPA: I like all this lazing around for profit and grandeur.

NANNA: As for the scale of the favours you'll sell, get this straight – it's very important. You've got to be shrewd and weigh up the status of whoever wants them. Make sure that while you ask one man for dozens of ducats, you don't let those paying one or two slip through your net. Publicise your top prices and keep the bargains secret – someone who wants to pay one ducat can do so, but not a word; someone who gives you ten can blow his own trumpet, and at the end of the month the money hived off is a perk. A woman who won't sell herself for anything less than twenty ducats is like a window covered with cloth, torn by every little breeze. Now let me give you a little tip. My dear, if, while you're out hunting for nice fat pheasants, one comes close to your trap, don't frighten him by making a racket, but hold your breath until he falls in – once he's caught, pluck his arse bare, while he's still halfway between life and death.

PIPPA: I don't understand.

NANNA: I mean that if you find a man of substance at your feet, don't scare him by asking for the moon, but take what he gives you; then, once he's ensnared, skin him alive – the same way a card-sharp will pretend to lose and let his opponent win a few hands, then cheat him to his heart's content.

PIPPA: I'll do the same.

NANNA: Never waste time, Pippa. Keep yourself busy around the house, sew a few stitches for the sake of appearances, work on your draperies, play a little tune you've learnt for fun, hammer at the clavichord, strum the lute, pretend to be reading *Furioso*, Petrarch, and the *Centonovelle*,[25] which you should always have on the table; show yourself at the window, then move away again; think and think about the art of whoredom. And if you don't feel like doing anything, lock yourself in your room and, mirror in hand, teach yourself how to blush artfully, and all the gestures,

83

mannerisms and movements you should use when laughing or crying, and how to lower your eyes and raise them when you need to.

PIPPA: What subtleties.

NANNA: Also – you know the rascally jargon of an utterly rascally rascal? Don't have any time for it and don't listen to anyone who does, or you'll almost certainly be regarded as one of their sort, and you'll never be able to open your mouth without arousing everyone's suspicions; and though I'll allow you to play tricks when appropriate, and on some of the Good Lord's creations you'd rather not see again, I won't accept you using slang on any account.

PIPPA: A nod's as good as a wink.

NANNA: I'm not going to tell you how to get yourself out of a pickle with excuses and retorts, because you're signalling me with your foot not to waste my breath telling you. So I'll do as you wish, and tell you instead that if you want to torment your lover, make sure that he doesn't suffer so much that he gets used to it, like a man who's carried the quartan fever for five or six years. Strike a happy medium and stick to the words of Serafino[26], who says:

> *Don't be too cruel, don't be too kind to lovers:*
> *They will either despair or be satiated.*

Don't show that your heart belongs so much to anyone, even if you care for them, that you can't give them a little hammer-blow on the anvil of their heart. And above all throw open the door to anyone who comes bearing gifts and bolt it against anyone who comes empty-handed. See to it that if someone sends you presents, he'll hear you saying to another who came with nothing: 'I like him so much that

I don't care for the others,' as if he wasn't there. Get cross with those you've offended before they get cross with you – they'll be overcome with love, and will say the *maxima culpa* for your own shortcomings. And if it so happens that you lose your temper with someone, don't wait too long before showing your anger, or you risk wasting the opportunity; anger is like the little hunger pang that's left when you're not completely full – it disappears when you leave the table, and nothing would tempt you to take another bite.

PIPPA: I know that feeling.

NANNA: Have I mentioned oaths to you?

PIPPA: Yes, but you contradicted yourself.

NANNA: I say things and then contradict myself – it's a woman's prerogative; we also say the same thing ten times, as I've probably already done.

PIPPA: You told me not to swear by God or the saints, and then you told me to swear an oath of loyalty to anyone who, out of jealousy, forbids me to have other lovers.

NANNA: That's true; swear, by all means, but not by God; it sounds bad enough coming out of the mouth of someone who's gambled his guts away, let alone a woman who's always winning.

PIPPA: I'll keep my mouth shut, then.

NANNA: Train your maid and valet to hint at some of your private little passions, while they're chatting with your lovers and you're in your room, and get them to say: 'Do you want to make the lady yours for good? Then buy her such-and-such a thing, because she's dying for it.' But make sure they don't ask for anything more than little tokens, like a bird in a gilded cage, or a little green parrot...

PIPPA: Why not a grey one?

NANNA: They're too expensive, and if you go that way, you

may well end up with nothing. Besides, now and then you can borrow whatever you want from one man or another, and take your time giving it back – if they don't ask for it, don't give it to them, because whoever's lent it to you will bide his time, brood over it and wait for your convenience. As you play for time, many of them will develop a sense of pride, and they'll be too embarrassed to send for something like a cape, a gown or a shirt or whatever it is, and you can often bag some nice little things.

PIPPA: I'd missed that one.

NANNA: I fished it up for you. Now, it's a fortnight before St Martin's[27]; and you call a little assembly of all of your lovers, and, sitting among them, use all the charms you know on them; then, when they're all drawn in by your simpering, say to them: 'I want us to play king of the bean[28]: until Carnival we'll each give a dinner, one after the other, starting with me, on the understanding that no one spends an arm and a leg, only a reasonable amount, just for a bit of fun.' This scheme is lots of fun and also very lucrative – there are many ways of making a profit. First of all, the dinner you give will come out of their purses; secondly, the 'king' has to sleep with you on the evening of his dinner and for that night His Majesty is required to pay royally; thirdly, the leftovers from each feast will last you a week, and, with a bit of pilfering, you'll get oil, firewood, wine, candles, salt, bread and vinegar. And if you can resell these extra provisions to someone or other on the quiet, go ahead, but if it gets out you'll get such a name that you'll struggle to find enough soap to clean it off, so perhaps it's best not to risk it.

PIPPA: Oh, that's a really good one.

NANNA: Now think of these words as priceless rubies – you can string them together like pearls. From time to time have your maid give you a lovebite on your neck or a little nip on the cheek with her teeth, to get the butterflies going in your lover's stomach as he imagines it was left there by his rival; also mess up your bed during the day, ruffle your hair and work a flush into your cheeks, but not too much; and, lo and behold, he'll huff and puff in his jealousy like a man who's caught his wife in flagrante delicto.

PIPPA: Got that one by heart.

NANNA: It'll do my own heart good if my advice bears fruit in your head, like wheat in the fields; but if it's been thrown to the wind, along with my suffering and despair will come your ruin, and in one week whatever money I leave you will have gone down the toilet. But if you do follow my advice, you'll be blessing your old mother's bones, flesh and dust, and you'll love her when she's gone as much as I think you love her now.

PIPPA: You can be sure of that, Mummy.

NANNA: Now, I'll break off here, and don't be moaning if I've given you more stuffing than meat; be happy I haven't told you even more.

'What more could you possibly want to tell me?' said Pippa to her mother. And she got up, stiff from sitting too long, and went yawning and stretching into the kitchen; and when supper was ordered, the knowledgeable little daughter, delighted at being able to open up shop, munched with relish at her food – she looked like a young girl whose father has promised to marry her off to her lover, so full of joy that she could hardly contain herself. And since one was worn out from talking and the other from listening, they went straight off to sleep in the same bed. And the following morning, waking up refreshed, they had breakfast when they wanted, and went back to the conversation.

Pippa had had a lovely dream around daybreak, and she began describing it to her mother, just as her mother was about to open her mouth and tell her about the betrayals that come from men's love...

NOTES

1. The conclave which elected Pope Leo X, Giovanni de' Medici (1475–1521), was held on 11th March 1513, therefore the dialogue is set in 1533. 'Balls, balls!' (a reference to the Medici's coat of arms) was the shout of Leo's supporters.

2. Syphilis.

3. Orlando (or Roland) is the hero of many chivalric epics, including, most famously, Ariosto's *Orlando Furioso* (1516–32).

4. St Nafissa is the imaginary sixteenth-century patron saint of prostitutes; Masetto da Lamporecchio is a character in Boccaccio's *Decameron* (3, 1), who, by pretending to be dumb, was appointed gardener in a convent, where he proceeded to conduct secret affairs with all the nuns.

5. Francesco Armellini Medici (1470–1528) was a noted cardinal from Perugia, who was very influential at the Roman Court; here his name is used purely as a Wellerism.

6. A work, originally printed in Venice in 1535, and attributed to Antonio Cavallino.

7. The 'mouth of truth' is a famous Roman monument in the shape of a face with an open mouth, situated in the porch of St Mary in Cosmedin. Superstition claims that if a person swears an oath while putting their hand into the mouth and the oath is false, then the hand will be bitten off.

8. 'Thirty-one' was a punishment dealt out to disobedient prostitutes; the prostitute in question was subjected to vaginal and anal sex by a group of thirty-one men.

9. Rienzo is used here as a typical Roman name.

10. The city of Rome was invaded and sacked by the Imperial army on 6th May 1527.

11. A mock usage of a standard ecclesiastical phrase.

12. In Dante's *Inferno*, heretics are punished in fiery tombs covered by inscribed tombstones which describe their various crimes.

13. It is still a popular belief in Italy that a pregnant woman's unsatisfied cravings result in a birthmark for the baby.

14. A supposed cure for syphilis.

15. The Gospels.

16. Troiano Pandolfini, Giovanni Lazzaro de Magistris (alias Serapica), and Francesco di Cazanigo da Milano (Acursio) were examples of people of humble origins who penetrated the inner circle of Leo X and Julius II.

17. Lift up your hearts.

18. Castruccio Castracani (1281–1328) was ruler of Lucca and a particularly formidable general. The expression used here was proverbial in Aretino's day.

19. Ancroia, an ugly old woman, was a stock character in many thirteenth-century French and fifteenth-century Italian burlesques.

20. The Collegio della Sapienza, or Collegio Capranica, was a board of theological and canonical studies, founded in 1457 by Cardinal Domenico Capranica (1400–58).

21. Psalms 51, 6 and 101 respectively.

22. In public.

23. Two popular gambling card games.

24. St Cosma and St Damiano are the patron saints of medicine, and were believed to have therapeutic powers.

25. *Furioso* is a reference to Ariosto's *Orlando Furioso*; the *Centonovelle* is another name for Boccaccio's *Decameron*.

26. Serafino Aquilano (1466–1500) was a Petrarchan poet and courtier who influenced the young Aretino.

27. St Martin's Day is 11th November.

28. The game involved drawing lots; and whoever drew the bean was named 'king', and had to put on a lavish party.

Pietro Aretino was born in Arezzo – from which he took his name – in 1492, the son of a cobbler. Very little is known of Aretino's early childhood, and it is possible that he had no formal education, though by the age of twenty he is known to have been living in Perugia, possibly as a student of art, where his first poems were written.

In 1517, he moved to Rome, where he lived with the wealthy patron Agostino Chigi, and became known at the Court of Pope Leo X. Here Aretino began writing satirical pieces, based on Court gossip and political affairs, and soon came to the notice of the papal aspirant Cardinal Giulio de' Medici. Giulio became his patron for a brief time during the conclave of 1521, in the hope that Aretino might enhance his chances of election by attacking his rival candidates. Both patron and poet were disappointed, however, by the election of the conservative Pope Adrian VI.

After this disappointment, Aretino moved away from Rome to Mantua for a time and sought new patrons, including the mercenary leader Giovanni de' Medici ('dalle Bande Nere'). He returned to Rome in 1523, when Giulio was elected Pope Clement VII, but was forced to leave briefly the following year after the publication of *I Sonetti Lussuriosi*, a collection of sonnets based on pornographic engravings by Giulio Romano. Aretino's popularity and notoriety grew, and he continued to circulate his satirical poetry and polemic letters – for which Ariosto gave him the title 'Scourge of Princes' – and, in 1525, completed his popular comedy *La Cortigiana* ['The Courtesan']. In 1527, however, he was forced to leave Rome permanently, when an assassin of Bishop Giovanni Giberti, one of his satiric targets, stabbed and almost killed him.

Aretino moved to Venice, where he spent the rest of his life, and where he produced the majority of his writings, including the *Ragionamento* [*Conversation*] (1534), and *Dialogo* [*Dialogue*] (1536), and the plays *Il Marescalco* ['The Farrier'] (1533) and *La Talanta* (1542). He continued to be a prolific letter-writer and was able to live partly on the income provided by the placatory gifts of his correspondents and targets, including, in 1533, King Francis I of France, who presented him with a gold chain. Aretino died in Venice, probably from an apoplectic fit, in 1556.

Rosa Maria Falvo lives in Italy and Australia as a teacher and translator. She is dedicated to developing and promoting intercultural and artistic exchange by fostering a wider appreciation for the language of the arts. Her published translations and introductions represent works from a variety of Italian artists.

HESPERUS PRESS – 100 PAGES

Hesperus Press, as suggested by the Latin motto, is committed to bringing near what is far – far both in space and time. Works written by the greatest authors, and unjustly neglected or simply little known in the English-speaking world, are made accessible through new translations and a completely fresh editorial approach. Through these short classic works, each around 100 pages in length, the reader will be introduced to the greatest writers from all times and all cultures.

For more information on Hesperus Press, please visit our website: **www.hesperuspress.com**

ET REMOTISSIMA PROPE

SELECTED TITLES FROM HESPERUS PRESS

Author	Title	Foreword writer
Jane Austen	*Love and Friendship*	Fay Weldon
Giovanni Boccaccio	*Life of Dante*	A.N. Wilson
Charlotte Brontë	*The Green Dwarf*	Libby Purves
Mikhail Bulgakov	*The Fatal Eggs*	Doris Lessing
Giacomo Casanova	*The Duel*	Tim Parks
William Congreve	*Incognita*	Peter Ackroyd
Gabriele D'Annunzio	*The Book of the Virgins*	Tim Parks
Dante Alighieri	*New Life*	Louis de Bernières
Marquis de Sade	*Incest*	Janet Street-Porter
Charles Dickens	*The Haunted House*	Peter Ackroyd
F. Scott Fitzgerald	*The Rich Boy*	John Updike
E.M. Forster	*Arctic Summer*	Anita Desai
D.H. Lawrence	*The Fox*	Doris Lessing
Leonardo da Vinci	*Prophecies*	Eraldo Affinati
Nikolai Leskov	*Lady Macbeth of Mtsensk*	Gilbert Adair
Niccolò Machiavelli	*Life of Castruccio Castracani*	Richard Overy
Francis Petrarch	*My Secret Book*	Germaine Greer
Luigi Pirandello	*Loveless Love*	
Alexander Pope	*Scriblerus*	Peter Ackroyd
François Rabelais	*Pantagruel*	Paul Bailey
François Rabelais	*Gargantua*	Paul Bailey
Italo Svevo	*A Perfect Hoax*	Tim Parks
Mark Twain	*The Diary of Adam and Eve*	John Updike
Giovanni Verga	*Life in the Country*	Paul Bailey
Jules Verne	*A Fantasy of Dr Ox*	Gilbert Adair
Oscar Wilde	*The Portrait of Mr W.H.*	Peter Ackroyd
Virginia Woolf	*Carlyle's House*	Doris Lessing
Virginia Woolf	*Monday or Tuesday*	Scarlett Thomas